GIRLS GETTING OFF

GIRLS GETTING OFF

A collection of 20 erotic stories

Edited by Elizabeth Coldwell

Published by Xcite Books Ltd – 2013

ISBN 9781908766274

Printed and bound in the UK

Cover design by Madamadari

Contents

Lady Blue
by Angela Goldsberry

It was a perfectly rotten end to a perfectly rotten day. I had spent my tenth wedding anniversary in a bar, drowning my sorrows in dirty martinis while my friends tried to console me over the fact that my bastard husband had left me for his big-titted, 20-something secretary. The icing on the cake: getting pulled over by the police on my way home. I knew why. I had blown a stop sign a few yards back. Normally, I wouldn't be nervous, but my breath smelled of vodka and it was Friday night. DUI patrols were out trawling for drunks. Just my luck.

'License, registration, and proof of insurance,' the patrolman requested curtly.

'I realise I missed the stop sign,' I said as I handed him my documentation. 'I didn't see it until I'd passed. There were tree branches in the way.'

The officer nodded noncommittally. 'Have you been drinking this evening, ma'am?'

'I had two martinis with dinner.' It wasn't strictly a lie. I did have two martinis with dinner. The fact that I had hadn't touched my food was another matter.

'I'm going to need you to step out of the car.'

Great. Yet another reason to curse my ex. While the officer murmured undecipherable police lingo into his radio, I opened the door of my little blue hatchback and fumbled about, trying to find my shoes. I couldn't stand driving in heels, so I always took them off. Floundering for them in the dark was not helping my case. Neither was the damned pencil skirt that impeded my getting out of the car. Finally, I got myself together enough to stand and face the patrolman, whose nametag read "Reynolds".

'Please walk ten paces up and back, one foot in front of the other,' he instructed.

No problem! Unless you're wearing five-inch spiked heels on a beat-up asphalt road. I twisted my ankle and stumbled on the seventh step. I would have fallen, had Reynolds not caught me.

'Whoa! Not doing so well, are we, Mrs Farnan?'

'*Miss*,' I retorted testily, bracing myself against his hard biceps as I regained my footing. Being rude wasn't smart, but I was still a little sensitive about my divorce. 'It's Miss Farnan,' I repeated in a more pleasant tone of voice.

'OK then, *Miss* Farnan. How about you come over here, off the road.'

He led me over to the passenger's side of his cruiser and backed me up against the rear door. It was probably police procedure, but he was a little too close for comfort.

'Turn around,' he said brusquely.

I did as I was told, forcing my numb body to turn towards the police cruiser. I could hear the dull metallic sound of handcuffs knocking against one another as Reynolds fished them out of his belt.

'We can do this the easy way or the hard way,' he said, clicking the handcuffs around my wrists. 'What'll it be?'

I could feel the bile rising in my throat as panic set in. This road was virtually deserted at night. I didn't stand a chance of fighting off a man of Reynolds' size. My mouth went dry and the air left my lungs.

'You want a breathalyzer, *Miss* Farnan?' His tone was mocking. 'I got something real nice for you to blow on.'

The quick blast of a siren prevented Reynolds from expounding on that thought. Another police cruiser flipped on its turret lights and pulled up behind him. A tall, red-headed woman in a police uniform exited the vehicle and made her way toward us. Reynolds muttered a curse under his breath and took a step back.

'Reynolds,' she called congenially, 'you know you're supposed to call for a female officer when you have a female search.'

'Uh, yeah, Sarge. I put in a call to dispatch. Didn't it go out?'

He did no such thing! I was about to call him on it, but he beat me to the punch.

'Let it go, *Miss* Farnan,' he cautioned in a low, gruff voice that intimated his ability to make my life a lot more miserable than I could make his.

'I didn't hear anything,' she said, rounding the back quarter panel of Reynolds' cruiser so that she was face to face with us. Her nametag read "Conwell".

'What do we have?' she asked, nodding her head at me, but not taking her emerald eyes off him.

'DUI,' he replied, squirming uncomfortably. 'I was just getting ready to transport her.'

Conwell eyed him a little suspiciously. 'Why don't I transport her for you?' she suggested.

I could feel Reynolds bristling. 'You gonna do all the paperwork too?'

Conwell nodded her head. 'Sure, Reynolds. I'll do the paperwork.'

Reynolds gave her a challenging glare, then thought better of it and released me from the cuffs. 'Tow truck's on its way,' he growled, handing her my information.

'That's fine,' Conwell said evenly as she grasped my upper arm gently.

'Aren't you going to cuff her?' Reynolds inquired testily.

'I don't think that's necessary.'

It seemed that Conwell was enjoying her subtle yet effective smackdown of Reynolds as much as I was. He was like an ill-tempered Doberman with a shock collar and a ten-inch leash. He couldn't say or do a thing, and he knew it.

Good dog, I thought smugly as we turned away from him, standing there, his furious eyes burning imaginary holes in our backs.

My arrogance over escaping a not-so-pleasant evening with Officer Reynolds was short-lived as it hit me: I was still being *arrested.*

'S-s-sergeant Conwell,' I stammered as she quietly led me to her car, 'if you'll let me explain –'

'Shhh,' she soothed, 'we'll talk in a minute. Let's get you out of here. Watch your step. You're likely to break your neck in those heels.'

She opened the rear door of her car and I obediently got in. What else was I going to do? Resist arrest? Not likely.

Sergeant Conwell retrieved my purse, nodded a polite goodnight to Officer Reynolds, and then climbed into the driver's seat of her car. She murmured some more police speak into her radio, then eased the cruiser onto the road. We passed Reynolds, leaning nonchalantly against the trunk of his cruiser, staring daggers at me. I had to resist the urge to flip him off.

'Did he hurt you?' Conwell asked, glancing at me in the rear-view mirror.

'No.' I didn't feel the need to tattle about Reynolds'

vulgar threat. I'd just as soon forget the whole thing. Besides, away from him it became clear: Reynolds was a bully, all bark and no bite. He'd forget about me before his shift was over.

'What's going to happen now?' I asked as Conwell pulled up in front of the tiny police station.

'Right now, I'm going to take you home.'

'But I thought –'

'That you were going to jail? For what? A drink or two with dinner?'

I nodded my head.

'You wouldn't have blown more than point zero three on a breathalyzer,' Conwell said, getting out of the car and opening my door. 'And while a designated driver would have been the prudent thing to do, you haven't broken any laws. I can't do anything about your car until morning, but I *can* give you a lift home.'

'I can get a cab.'

Conwell laughed. 'In this town? We have 24 cops and two cabs. You could walk home faster. Just let me sign out.'

I waited for her on a bench in the vestibule. The desk sergeant gave me a curious glance, then went back to his novel. Not a whole lot going on in East Podunk tonight, was there?

Not a whole lot happened on the short ride to my apartment either. We drove in silence except when I was giving directions. We pulled into the parking lot, where it was quiet, dark, and spooky.

'Thanks for bringing me home, Sergeant Conwell.'

'No problem. And it's Lucy.'

At the mention of her name, my eyes were drawn to her flaming red hair, even though I willed them not to be. The *I Love Lucy* theme song started playing in my head. I couldn't help it, it just did.

Lucy laughed and nodded. 'Yeah, Mom was a big fan.'

'Be glad you weren't a blonde. She might have named you Ethel.'

We both cringed, then burst out laughing. We laughed until we were out of breath. Then we fell silent.

'Well,' I said, a little uncomfortably, 'I should go.'

Lucy nodded. 'It was nice to meet you, Elise.'

I unbuckled my seatbelt and exited the low-slung coupe. I had not gone more than three steps when my ankle gave out on me – again! I might have laughed had I not been so fed up with life at the moment.

Lucy was at my side before I had a chance to get up. 'Are you OK?'

'I'm fine. This just hasn't been my day.' Suddenly, I was sobbing, telling Lucy everything about my horrible day, my horrible ex, and my horrible life. She listened to it all, letting me vent while she helped me up and into my apartment. I didn't even realise we'd gone inside until I felt Lucy press a warm, wet washcloth on my skinned knee. I wondered if I should be upset that she'd made herself at home, shedding her jacket, seeking out my linen closet for the washcloth, and raiding my freezer to pour me a double shot of vodka. I took a calming drink from the glass she handed me and decided I wasn't.

'The stockings are trashed, but otherwise, this doesn't look too bad,' Lucy said, lifting the cloth from my knee. She gently blew on the scrape, cooling the burn. A little shiver went up my spine.

Lucy lifted my leg, trying to inspect my ankle as she knelt on the carpet. 'I can't get a good look at this. Get rid of the stockings so we can see whether or not you should go to the ER.'

'I'm sure it's not that bad,' I said dismissively. I had

already inconvenienced her enough for one night.

'Probably not, but let's make sure.'

Too weary to argue, I stood up, trying not to put any weight on my ankle, unzipped my skirt, and shimmied out of it. I grabbed the waistband of my hose and pushed the nylon over my hips and down to my thighs. My fingers brushed Lucy's as she took over, sliding the hose down to my ankles. No need for modesty amongst girls, right? Suddenly, I felt exposed and embarrassed. I might as well have been naked, standing before her, my lace-clad crotch level with her face. I quickly dropped onto the couch, and nonchalantly crossed my hands over my lap.

'What do you think?' I asked Lucy, trying to relax. But inside, I was live wire. My nipples were like diamonds as they rubbed against the lace of my bra. My panties were soaked. I was totally turned on.

'I think you'll live,' she said, gingerly palpating my inner ankle. There was minimal swelling and no bruising. She pressed her fingers against the tender spot and began to rub in a slow, rhythmic motion. Again, I felt a surge of arousal course through my pelvis. I dismissed it; I was misinterpreting Lucy's intentions. But there could be no mistake when Lucy pressed her lips to the spot she had been rubbing. She looked at me expectantly as her tongue slipped out from between her lips and began to trace circles around my ankle. She was waiting for permission. A flash of the eyes and an imperceptible nod of the head marked my consent.

Lucy slowly licked her way from my ankle to my knee, gently parting my legs and climbing between them. A few scant inches separated our faces and I could feel her dewy breath on my skin.

Then she kissed me. Her lips felt like rose petals, velvety and smooth. My mouth was pliant beneath hers, lips spreading eagerly at the urging of her tongue. Lucy slipped her hands under my ass, pulling me forward, pressing my body against hers, spreading my legs wide.

As our tongues slid over one another, I undid the braid that held her fiery tresses captive. Lucy freed the buttons of my blouse and palmed my breasts, kneading them through my bra, softly at first, then with more urgency when she heard my whimper of pleasure. I managed to pull her uniform shirt free from her pants and made quick work of the buttons. Her shirt found a home on the floor with mine.

Without further ado, she reached behind her, loosened the clasps of her plain, cotton work bra. What lay beneath was anything but plain. Her double Ds jutted out at me, looking delicious, daring me to touch. And I did. They were the first breasts – aside from my own – that I'd ever touched. Handling them was a newfound, sexy delight. They were warm and firm in my hands as I squeezed them, holding their weight in my palms, brushing the nipples with my thumbs. Lucy moaned appreciatively.

In gratitude, she pulled down the lace cups of my bra and sucked one of my nipples into her mouth, swirling her tongue around the hardened tip. When I leant back to shove more of my petite breast into her mouth, my precariously perched rear slid off the sofa and onto her lap. The cold leather of Lucy's holster dug into my thigh, but I didn't care. I was preoccupied with the buckle, its hard steel flicking against my engorged clit when I swivelled my hips.

'Not yet,' Lucy admonished seductively. 'We have things to do.'

Such as? My interest was definitely piqued.

She rose up on her knees, pushing me back onto the couch. Her fingers curled around the lace of my panties, pulling them off. She spread my knees wide again, sliding her hands up my thighs until they met on either side of my swollen pussy. With delicate precision, she used her thumbs to part the golden curls, opening my folds like the pages of a book.

'God, you're so wet!' she exclaimed, rubbing up and down my slit with the pad of her thumb. I couldn't help but moan. Lucy slid her thumb all the way down my wet gash and slowly pushed it inside me. I moaned louder.

'Is that good?' she asked, drawing her thumb out and then easing it back in.

'Yes!'

Lucy continued to fuck me with her thumb, sliding in and out of me at an unhurried pace. It was an exquisite torture.

'More?' she offered.

'Please,' I croaked.

She bent her head and added her mouth, her wet tongue gliding over my pussy like a skater on ice while her thumb stayed its course. She affixed her lips to my tingling clit, sucking on it and releasing it every time my hips rose.

She giggled at my obvious eagerness. 'Which way to the bedroom?'

'That way.'

Lucy grabbed my hand and we ran down the hall, stopping twice for her to press me up against the cool walls, fondling and kissing me, until we fell through the open doorway. A small lamp shone; a soft glow that was perfect for seduction. *My* seduction. At the hands of a lady in blue. A cop sex fantasy come true.

My heart was in my throat as I climbed onto the queen-sized bed.

'Oh!' Lucy exclaimed. 'Stop right there!'

I froze in mid-crawl, on my hands and knees with my back – or should I say *ass* – to Lucy. I could feel the mattress depress under her weight as she came up behind me.

'I couldn't help but notice this,' she said, smoothing her hands over my curved rear, 'when you were on your knees out front.'

'Oh really?' I giggled.

'*Really.*'

She quickly discarded the rest of her clothes. I held my pose for her, watching her over my shoulder. She reinforced her approval by pressing her lips to each of my rounded cheeks. Her breath was hot and moist as she zeroed in on the vertical smile between my legs. She buried her face in my pussy, driving her tongue deeply into me. Her nose pressed enticingly against my crease and, when she joined me on the bed, she let her tongue trail upward and punctuate the hot, pink pucker there, tonguing me until I begged her to stop.

She fell back onto the mattress and looked at me, her beryl eyes glinting in the dim light. 'Stop? But, Elise, we're just getting started.'

Boldly, I crawled over to her and straddled her hips. 'Are we now?'

Lucy purred like a kitten as I lowered my pussy onto hers. I ground my wet lips against her hard mound, instinctively knowing that she would like it. Grabbing her lovely tits, I squeezed them hard as I rode her. Her hips bucked off the mattress, the word "yes" dripping from her lips, a barely audible mantra that was as much a plea as an affirmation. She was on the brink of orgasm, and I had a front row seat. I dismounted and crawled between her thighs. Her musky scent tickled my nose, drawing me in to taste the tangy juice that dribbled out of her pussy. I was a novice, but it was easy as pie. Sweet pussy pie. I knew what I liked; not coincidentally, Lucy liked it too. Intuition and the whimpering noises that Lucy made whenever I hit a particularly sensitive spot kept me on the right path.

I swept my tongue up and down her pussy in slow, broad strokes, cleaving her puffy, shaved lips so I could service her clit. I worked that knot over, sucking and pulling on it with my lips, circling and flicking it with my tongue.

Lucy snaked her hands between her legs and she pulled her lips as far apart as she could. 'More,' she gasped, as my tongue darted in and out of her slippery hole.

I worked one finger into her, and then another, and then a third. She was tight and hot, growing wetter and wetter as my fingers worked their magic.

'Oh, oh, *ohhh*!' she cried as she came, her pussy clamping down on my hand. I stayed with her, humming triumphantly as I sucked on her clit. She came again almost immediately, and I had to admit, I was fairly impressed with myself.

'Come here,' Lucy whispered breathlessly.

I slid up on the sheets until we were side by side. Lucy kissed me, softly lapping at my lips, cheeks, and chin, tasting herself on my face, cooing with pleasure. As she was winding down, I was winding up, and we became a tangle of arms and legs, lips and tongues, wrestling on the bed.

Lucy rolled me onto my back and held my hands over my head. Drawing one of my nipples up between her lips, Lucy sucked and nipped at the hardened pebble with her teeth and tongue until it was just shy of painful.

'You like that, don't you? Well, then how about this?' She slid backward and hooked my legs over her thighs.

She plunged two fingers into my slick channel. The wet, sucking noises my drenched pussy made while Lucy fingered me were a beautiful accompaniment to the crescendo of my moans. She needed no answer. The proof was in the pussy.

I tugged on my nipples while Lucy tapped out a Morse code on my G-spot; the more I tugged, the more she tapped, the wetter I got. Two fingers, three fingers, four. The way Lucy filled and stretched my tight pussy made me want to die. I held on, panting and moaning, while she encouraged me with her sweetly murmured dirty talk.

'That's it,' she crooned as I gyrated my hips, 'your pussy looks so pretty with my fingers in it. So pink and wet. I can't wait to feel you come. Will you come for me, Elise? Will you?'

I nodded. She had no idea how badly I wanted to. But orgasm eluded me, always just out of reach.

'What do you need, baby? Tell me how to make you come.'

Quickly, I scrambled to my knees.

Lucy smiled knowingly. 'Mmmm,' she said coming up behind me, 'you want a little something back here too, don't you?'

'Please,' I implored.

'Always happy to protect and serve.' She pushed on my shoulders so that I was face down on the bed, my ass in the air. Dipping her thumb into my pussy, she coated it with slippery juice and smeared it up and down my crease. The tight rosette of my ass winked at her as she circled it slowly on the outside with her thumb. Gently, she pressed against the muscle, patiently waiting until it gave way and sucked her in up to the second knuckle.

'Oh God,' I groaned, millions of nerve endings in my ass applauding its welcome invader. I thought I might faint, but I didn't. My body became electrified, sparking and jumping at every touch, giving me goosebumps.

Wow, I thought, just wow. I had my lover's thumb pistoning in and out of my ass – a taboo treat that I'd only dreamt about before now – as her fingers wriggled against the tight walls of my pussy. Not one to sit by idly, I kept myself busy, pinching and rolling my throbbing clit. Rocking back and forth against Lucy's hands, I was on a roller coaster of pleasure, teetering at the apex of orgasm, ready to thunder down the other side.

'This is what you need, isn't it, baby?' Lucy said in a whisper. 'For someone to fuck your hot little ass? It's so tight! Am I your first?'

I couldn't speak. A little squeak of affirmation was the best I could manage. I used to privately sing the praises of the vibrating plug I kept in my dresser, like it was the best thing since beltless maxi pads. News flash: it couldn't hold a candle to Lucy.

She worked her other thumb into my ass, diving and retreating with its partner, stretching the tight orifice more than I'd ever dared. I furiously rubbed my swollen clit until, finally, in an incredible, repeating, pulsating rush, I came. Hard. To say I saw stars was an understatement.

I collapsed onto the bed and Lucy came with me, snuggling up, her head on the pillow next to me. She entwined her legs with mine and cupped my still-throbbing pussy possessively with her hand. I toyed with her breasts, kneading them gently.

'You're quite the little criminal,' she teased as I ran circles around the taut, dusky peaks with my thumbs. 'I think you broke three or four laws there – at least.'

I blushed. 'It was a conspiracy! I had an accomplice!'

Lucy laughed. 'I won't tell, if you won't.'

Then she kissed me, her slippery tongue caressing

mine with sensual expertise. I could feel her fingers nudging my sticky lips apart, pushing their way into my syrupy opening.

'This is the police,' she breathed into my mouth as she started to work my pussy again. 'Spread 'em.'

Burmese Bells and Retro Rockets
by Encarnita Round

Sasha waltzed into my office, perched herself on the end of the desk and waited for me to speak. I didn't; I was busy. It didn't matter to Sasha that I was typing up the minutes of the last meeting: when Sasha wanted your attention then your attention is what she got.

'Hi, honey,' she said, interrupting my flow, 'what are you doing tomorrow night?'

'Nothing,' I answered distractedly as I reread the sentence I'd just typed.

'As your best friend,' she went on, 'it's my duty to make sure that you don't turn into a sour puss.'

'Right,' I answered, and saved the file just in case.

She leant over and bounced my left boob in her hands. 'When was the last time you took those babies out to play?'

I shrugged. She was in one of those moods. 'How's Dave?' I asked instead; that always changed the subject.

'Dumped,' she answered cheerfully, 'but that's not important, you are. So I've decided that tomorrow night you can come to a girls' night with me.'

That got my attention. 'What, with strippers?'

'No, not that sort of girls' night.' She laughed, 'We're going out, to a "girls' night in" at a friend's house.'

'I'd rather watch paint dry,' I said and turned back to

my computer.

'Oh Annie, we'll have a great time. You'll love it, trust me.'

I stared at her through narrowed eyes, because she was clearly up to something. 'Sasha –' I decided on the direct route. 'What's the catch?'

'No catch,' she assured me. 'We'll have such a great night, you'll see.'

I was not convinced. 'I think there's a spot of paint that I need to keep an eye on.'

Sasha laughed. 'I'll be at your house at six. Get yourself dressed up, and bring something to drink.'

'What? Horlicks?'

Sasha giggled. 'Only if it has vodka in it.'

'But what if I don't want to go …?'

'You will. Six o'clock tomorrow night. No excuses.' Before I could think of anything to say she was off, out of my space and into her own office. Just as quickly, I forgot all about it. Yes, we were friends, but when it came to it, when it came to a Friday night, I didn't think I would be high on Sasha's list of priorities. Even if I was, Sasha was easily distracted by something that sounded like more fun, so I took the whole thing with a huge pinch of salt and paid it no more thought at all.

When the knock came, at precisely six, I wasn't really expecting her to be the one doing the knocking. I was even more surprised at how she was dressed. Sasha didn't wear skirts; she wore belts that rarely covered her arse, and tops that only just concealed the nipples. A skirt that reached to mid-thigh and a blouse that showed just a hint of cleavage made her look smart and sexy in a restrained, not-really-Sasha kind of way.

'Wow!' I said. 'You have a date? A serious date?'

'Get away. Aren't you ready yet?' she replied without really answering, but she was pleased at my response, I could tell that much.

'As ready as I am going to be,' I said as I looked down at my old and worn jeans. They fitted beautifully, even if I did say so myself. Best of all, they were incredibly comfortable, as was the plain white V-neck T-shirt I'd opted for. 'A night "in" with a bunch of women I hardly know?' Wasn't exactly a night at the opera, now was it?

Sasha shook her head, tutted and tsked at every part of my attire that warranted her disapproval. 'You really need to go out more, honey.'

'I do go out.' I insisted as usual, but Sasha's idea of a good time is not the same as mine.

'At least change your top to something that shows off your knockers. You shouldn't hide 'em away like that.'

So I did. Don't know why, but it seemed the best thing to do. At least she stopped moaning so much. She looked me over once more, and even with my boobs more prominently displayed, she still managed to tut with disapproval. 'Never mind, it'll do. You'll feel much better after this, I am sure.' I wasn't sure of anything, of course.

At least it wasn't hard to find number 72 Wishbourne Avenue. Unmissable, the house was the only one with a huge banner strung between two of the upstairs windows. It said, in bright pink letters two foot high, "Girls' Night In". As I said, hard to miss.

Sasha didn't even knock at the front door; she pushed it open and headed straight for the kitchen where they stashed the important things, like the wine. Sasha knew everyone, but although I was treated courteously, I felt just like the ugly mate who got tagged on by mistake. Interestingly, I thought, they were all dressed to impress, and I admit I felt less than comfortable, but not so much

17

that I worried about it. Sasha vanished almost the moment we entered the kitchen; as I eyed up the other women, I could hear her unmissable giggle echo from the lounge. Like I said, Sasha is easily distracted by the prospect of more fun elsewhere.

'Hello,' said the woman standing next to me. 'You've been abandoned, I take it?'

'Looks that way,' I responded dryly over the rim of my glass and not really paying her that much attention. Well, not until I heard her throaty chuckle, which sounded so downright dirty that I had to look. I was transfixed. Was it because she was stunning? Was it because she looked darkly exotic, with olive skin, and brown eyes so deep and dreamy they smouldered? Perhaps it was something simpler, like the fact that although she dressed it all up in plain black leggings and a long, sleeveless top, there was no hiding the woman underneath. It was all of these things, I think, but when my eyes settled on her full and luscious lips, lips that begged to be kissed, I felt a surging response. I gulped the rest of my wine, and hoped that no one noticed when I squeezed my legs together.

'I'm Alex, by the way,' she said in a surprisingly soft voice, 'and welcome to my home.'

'Thank you,' I responded, my legs gripped together so tightly it was almost painful.

'Your first visit, isn't it?'

I nodded, and tried to focus my attention on my glass.

'Not to worry,' she said. Mistaking my reticence, she put her hand on my arm and squeezed pure electricity along every nerve ending I possessed. 'It'll be fine once you've relaxed. Just go with the flow.' Oh, I was flowing all right, but probably not in the way that she intended. 'Still, if you are unsure of anything, just call for me.' She excused herself then and, with just one last meaningful glance over her shoulder, she was swallowed up by the other women.

Back to being on my own again, I thought as I heard Alex in the room next door.

'All right, I know you're impatient,' she announced, 'Shall we get started?'

One minute the kitchen was lively, full of expectation, and then the next it was completely empty. Intrigued, I followed the other guests into the lounge, where they all squeezed together on the available seats. There was no room for me by then, but I didn't mind overly; I was just as happy to lean against the door frame and watch things unfold. I still couldn't see what all the fuss was about.

One thing I did notice was Sasha, sitting on the floor with her back between the knees of a woman I'd not met before. They were intimately entwined, with Sasha's arms around the woman's legs as her fingers traced lazy circles over exposed ankles. I watched, like a voyeur, catching a glimpse of a life otherwise hidden. She looked up then, and caught my eye. Seeing my quizzical expression, she simply smiled girlishly and shrugged. Obviously I didn't know Sasha as well as I thought.

'So glad you could all make it,' the hostess announced smoothly and confidently. 'I think we can safely say that we all know each other very well.' She laughed then, and everyone laughed with her. 'But we do have a new face in the house, so a few introductions are in order. I'm Alex, the party organiser, and my partner in crime is my next-door neighbour, Pam.'

The woman sitting behind Sasha raised her hand. 'That's me,' she said.

'And you obviously know Sasha. She's the one who's staked her place between Pam's legs. Again.' Everyone laughed, and Alex winked at me. 'There's Claire –' and

Claire put her hand in the air '– Sam, Netty, Nicole, Chris, Jo, and Maria.'

Each one made herself known. They were a mixed bunch of women, which was interesting in itself, but I was more than aware that their appraisal was a little direct; I should have dressed up after all.

'Come on girls,' Alex started, 'you can make our guest more welcome than that. It's her first time, so let's make Annie a part of the group, shall we?' Claire and Netty jumped up and, moments later, I was on the sofa and wedged between the two of them. That was it, stuck, and pleasantly so. The heat of the two women warming my sides, and their arms interlinked with mine, I felt as though I belonged there.

'Have you looked at the sideboard?' Netty whispered to me.

I shook my head; I was concentrating on Alex in her leggings. I had such a lovely view of her fabulous rear anything else just wasn't worth even thinking about.

'Stop ogling Alex. She doesn't play, you know,' Netty whispered, and pointed. 'Look at the sideboard.'

In most houses, the sideboard is the place to find dining-related paraphernalia: plates, the cutlery canteen, napkins, that sort of thing. In this house, Alex had the top lined with vibrators, and other toys, not entirely suited to the average dinner party. A rail of clothing stood in the corner, but I doubted if those *costumes* would be found in the local Marks.

'The rules of the house are simple,' Alex said. 'Have a good time, no dramas, and the kitchen is a neutral zone. Got that?'

Everyone nodded, so I did too.

'What's a neutral zone?' I asked Netty.

'Shh,' she responded.

'Last time,' Alex started as she grabbed various items from the sideboard, 'we discussed and demonstrated Ben Wa balls, Kegels, love eggs, jiggle balls, Burmese bells, Venus balls, toner balls … Whatever you call 'em, they are essentially the same thing.' She held up a few so that we could all see. 'How'd we get on? Claire, you bought a set from me, want to start?'

Claire, probably in her early 40s and dressed a little more conservatively than most, stood up. 'Oh yes, I do like my jiggle balls!' She grinned at Alex. 'Wonderful. Only take them out to wash them.' Then she giggled. 'Yes, I need to buy another pair.'

Alex clapped her hands delightedly. 'I am so pleased. You're tightening the muscles too?'

'Oh, and then some.' Claire laughed raucously and an energetic discussion of Kegels ensued. The way the discussion was going it looked as though a demonstration was likely. Claire was more than willing if anyone wanted to take a look.

My eyes turned to Pam and Sasha, and I watched as Pam massaged Sasha's scalp with her fingertips. Sasha liked it; she closed her eyes and moaned almost too quietly to hear. I knew she did, though, probably the moment Pam touched her ears, her throat, and her hand crept inside the top of her blouse.

'And tonight's topic is –' Alex paused, oblivious to the goings-on '– dildos.' She looked in my direction. I guess she had no idea how I would react, being new and all.

'But I have a man for that,' Claire offered, almost indignantly. 'Except when he's tired, and then I have my Rabbit.'

Several of the women squealed.

'Ahh, Claire,' Alex said, 'what would we do without you?'

Claire shrugged expansively.

'All I can say is pegging is the new thing that men, some men, are really into. So have you asked him if he would like to be screwed? And wouldn't you like to be the one who gives him one?'

'Err...' Claire faltered and Alex launched into her discussion. I admit I did find it fascinating. Not just the subject, but Alex too. Most people just wave their hands when they talk; Alex used her entire body and it was riveting. When she pulled a harness over her leggings and put a multi-coloured fake member in place, everyone took notice.

'This is my Retro Rocket.' She smirked. 'It glows in the dark, it's colourful, fun, and a fabulous ride, even if I do say so myself.'

I think everyone in the room leant closer, especially when she demonstrated her moves. 'It's a great addition to any toy collection, for the boys or the girls, and does pretty much anything you can do with a vibrator, only hands free.' She winked. 'And I do like to be hands free.'

It was a great discussion and my head was filled to bursting with Alex, the way she moved, and being hands free. Then it was all over and people got up and mingled; some headed for the display, and some disappeared. Sasha went into the conservatory with Pam, and the sliding door closed with a degree of deliberation and finality. Then they closed the curtains from their side, and we were all excluded. Except for the gap at one end, and when I saw Pam wrap her arms around Sasha I knew I would not look away, not unless I had to.

'Did you enjoy that?' Alex asked, her grin broad and inviting.

I assumed that she meant the talk rather than my view. 'Very informative,' I answered, and pointed to the multi-coloured piece of silicon that was pointing from her groin. 'I think you might want to remove that before you impale someone.'

'Maybe that's the idea.'

'Right.'

'Oh, I don't impale just anyone, you know.'

'Really?'

'Really.' Alex laughed. 'You're not what I expected.'

I didn't ask what she meant by that, as she grabbed my hand and almost dragged me closer to the display. Once again, I didn't really listen much as my eyes were drawn to the gap in the curtains; the view was better from this position. Sasha, already half naked, sat on a wicker armchair, skirt pulled up around her waist, and her blouse on the floor. Her legs were spread, each one draped over the arms of the chair, and Pam knelt between them. She was lapping away, holding Sasha still as she feasted, and Sasha, her head thrown back, enjoyed it all.

It was a while before I remembered Alex was standing next to me, saying not a word. 'Oh my,' I whispered. It had been a while since I remembered being in such an aroused state, and I was jealous. A part of me wondered whether Sasha would mind if I joined in.

'Nice, isn't it?' Alex commented, bringing me back to the here and now, and the steady throb that pulsed between my legs.

'Yes, lucky for some.'

'So,' Alex started as she ran a finger along my bare arm, 'does anything take your fancy?'

If her hand earlier had felt like electricity, now a single finger felt like a thousand volts pushed between my legs. Even my knees went weak, and I had to really concentrate to avoid groaning. I turned to Alex. 'Yes, but what takes my fancy doesn't come in a box.'

'Oh naughty.' Alex smirked. 'So you wouldn't be interested in any toys, then?'

'Perhaps,' I whispered, 'but only if you demonstrate their use to the fullest extent.'

Alex took a step closer and my heart raced. 'I could do that,' she whispered, 'but unlike those two in there, I like more privacy.'

'You're not a watcher, then?' I asked as I turned back towards Sasha. In those minutes that I had focused on Alex, the scene in the conservatory had changed. Sasha was naked now, apart from a leather harness, the straps around her waist and reaching between her legs. She had her own rocket; not a psychedelic retro one, but a bright pink thing. It looked huge.

I felt Alex step behind me, and although she stood really close, she wasn't close enough to touch. Pity. Instead, I focused on Sasha, getting a view of a world that was not mine. Pam, naked, lying on the rug on the floor, looked flushed and ready. She reached out to Sasha, and although I could not hear the words, I could see her lips move. 'Come to me, baby,' I am sure she said, and Sasha did. She knelt between the woman's legs, lifted Pam's hips, and guided herself into position. I saw Pam nod expectantly, and then Sasha rammed the pink cock home. Even though the door was closed, I could hear the howl of delight as she was filled with Sasha's thrust.

'Hmmm,' I whispered as I watched, unable to move away, as Sasha lay on top of Pam and they started to rock together. Pam's legs hooked around Sasha's thighs, pinning her in place, and all I could see was Sasha's arse as she pumped away. She had great rhythm and watching her was almost hypnotic, and definitely hot. I was hot.

Alex stepped closer, and she slipped her arms around my waist. 'Enjoying the show?' she whispered into my ear, her breath warming the side of my face. A shiver raced along my spine; the other thing affecting me was the feel of the rocket pressing against my rear.

'Oh yes,' I answered, not caring if I was supposed to watch, never mind enjoy it. I leant backwards so that I could feel more of Alex, and wiggled my hips in the hope of getting better contact. She tightened her arms around me and her lips brushed against the back of my neck. I tried not to moan, but I am not sure I managed it.

'Alex.' I mumbled, and she turned me around, not letting me go for a second. Face to face, I could look into her eyes, her pupils so dilated with desire that her eyes looked almost black. When she pressed herself firmly against me, her hips moved slightly but suggestively, and the rocket sawed into me. It was a promise, and I liked that kind of promise. I kissed her, lightly and a little tentatively. She smiled, momentarily, an almost distracted look on her face, but her responding kiss was a bruising possession of my mouth. I liked that. The heat between my legs let me know I liked that a lot.

Welded together, by touch, by kisses, Alex started to walk backwards, out of the dining room, through the kitchen and into the hallway. It was slow progress as we never parted, not even for a second, and each inelegant step took us lurching through her house. Continuous, demanding, and relentless kisses kept me short of breath and I ignored the other women, their pairings. All I could think of was her hands inside my blouse, gripping my hot skin and driving me almost wild with anticipation. By the time we hit the bottom of the stairs Alex could wait no longer, and I was pushed against the wall. My jeans were unfastened and loosely hanging from my hips as she tried to get her hand inside. 'Upstairs,' I breathed, but only because I wanted a little more privacy and didn't want to be disturbed by anyone or anything. We bounded up the stairs two steps at a time, and wasted no more time at all.

I hardly noticed the decor of the bedroom, all of my attention was focused on Alex. Her top was soon thrown to the floor, and that left her chest open to my eyes and to my hands. I grabbed her by the Retro Rocket, which she still wore, and as it shamelessly pointed the way, I pulled her until she was within striking distance.

She laughed, that throaty and dirty laugh that she had, and she pushed me onto the bed.

'Get your clothes off,' she ordered and, as I complied, she unstrapped her harness, and stripped herself bare.

I was disappointed. I thought Alex, the rocket, and I could get acquainted.

'I know what you want,' she leered, 'but you'll have to wait. Lean back and let me see you.'

I did as I was told.

'Spread them further,' she ordered as she crawled, naked, onto the bed and on top of me. I pulled her against me, kissed her, invaded her mouth with my tongue, and squirmed until I pushed her off. 'I'll be top, shall I?' I said, grinning.

'Only because I will let you,' she growled.

I said no more as I sat straddling her hips and wiggled to get my rear against her. She thought that funny too and, before I could move, her hand reached between my legs and she found me more than wet and ready. She slipped two fingers inside. 'Just being on top doesn't put you in charge,' she told me, and then added another finger. I felt so full of her, it was better than any rocket. She sat up, her head resting on my chest as she pumped her whole arm and the fingers nestled inside of me. I had to hold on, and wrapped my arms around her shoulders. I gripped hard as my hips thrust rhythmically against her hand, and the thumb that rested against the engorged shaft of my clit.

She waited, I think, till I was almost ready to explode, and then she withdrew. Without her fingers I felt empty, disappointed. She flipped me on to my back and pinned me to the bed as she nipped the base of my neck. 'Who's in charge now?' she whispered against my hot skin.

'You are, Alex, you are.'

She slipped lower, kissed my chest, and the attention to my breasts was divine. Her mouth was hot and wet on my nipples, but she did not linger. She kissed my stomach, nipped at my belly, and buried her face between my legs. She took a deep breath, taking in all of my scent, my arousal. 'Hmm,' she managed, then her mouth was on me, and I squirmed with pleasure as her nose pressed against my clit and her mouth surrounded my entrance. Her long and agile tongue just slipped inside. After just a few strokes of that soft and divine tool, my back arched, I clamped my thighs around her ears, and I came for her.

Alex did not stop there; after prising my legs apart she kissed all of my folds and skin with great gentleness. I was still on fire, and I knew she would not take long to build me up once more. 'Alex,' I called out and reached for her. When she looked up, her face glistened with the fruits of my pleasure. Even after she had wiped her face, I could still taste myself on her lips.

'My turn,' I said, but her eyes twinkled mischievously with the look of someone who has her own plans. 'Please let me,' I repeated.

'I want to fuck you,' she said simply. 'I want to get inside you again, and ride you until you squeal.'

That sounded so good. I almost let her. 'Later,' I soothed as I stroked the sides of her breasts. 'Right now I really want to please you, will you let me?'

She nodded as we lay on our sides, facing each other. I

like it fast, but I wanted to know Alex thoroughly and I explored her body slowly and gently. She liked what I did; her eyes never left my face, and her bravado and bossiness had vanished. I skimmed my fingertips over her breasts, her nipples, and she shivered with every touch. Her skin was so soft that I could stroke her for hours. I leant forward, took a nipple between my lips, and lashed the tip with my tongue. Alex stiffened and whimpered. When I took the nipple into my mouth I sucked, a little harder than normal, but Alex groaned loudly. She liked that.

Her skin was smooth over her hip, and her thighs were firm, the muscles beneath responding to my touch. Then I was between her legs, into her heat. She parted her legs for me, and positioned her limbs so that I gained easy and unobstructed access. I found her wetness, swirled my fingers tentatively around her clit, and she took my hand and guided two fingers inside. She pushed against my fingers slowly, her movements controlled and exact, and inside my fingers swirled against her inner walls.

All the time she looked into my eyes, her face serious, and giving nothing away. Other than her increasingly laboured breathing, the red flush creeping over her cheeks and throat, she seemed so contained.

I felt her orgasm in my fingers first. Her walls gripped my fingers so tightly and she bore into me with such force that she almost pushed me out. Her fingers dug into my hip as her eyes grew blurred and unfocused. She leant into me and half bit my shoulder to stifle her sounds. But I heard her anyway, a little, suppressed whimper that accompanied the tensions ripping through her body. She strained against me, shaking until there was no more left to give.

We fell asleep then, not for long. But we woke to the

sounds of the others yelling goodbye and good night. Alex stretched beside me. 'Did you enjoy your girls' night in?' she asked.

'Not what I expected at all.'

She grinned. 'So will you come along to the next one?'

I laughed at that. 'Only if you bring out your rocket.'

'I have something better than that,' she said. 'Stay with me a while longer.'

How could I say no? I couldn't.

Andie After All
by Landon Dixon

Jessica Taylor was one sexually frustrated young girl. As she lay back, rigid, on her bed, and furiously rubbed her clit and felt up her breasts, she replayed the recent shower scene in her mind over and over.

It'd seemed like the perfect time and place and setting to finally put the moves she'd been mentally practising for months on her classmate, Andie Perkins. The two high school seniors had been the last ones off the volleyball court, working on their bumping and setting skills at Coach Carlyle's belligerent behest. So that by the time they'd finally stripped down in the locker room and padded into the shower, all the other girls on the team had already finished up and gone home.

Jessica had stared longingly at Andie through the steamy mist, watching the green-eyed honey-blonde rub soap onto her gleaming, bronze body – over her buff shoulders and down her slender arms, in between and onto her lush breasts, around her darker, puffy nipples, across her flat stomach and into the dripping blonde fur of her pussy, over and onto and up and down her glistening, round, bouncy buttocks. It'd been quite a show. Jessica's throat had almost cracked with dryness, her tongue swollen, despite the hot, humid, dripping confines and the drooling of her open mouth.

But when she'd gulped up enough courage and saliva to finally croak, 'C-can I help r-rub your back?' Andie had squirmed away with a giggle.

'Don't be silly. I'm all done,' was all she'd said.

She was always teasing Jessica; whether innocently or deliberately, Jessica wasn't sure. Either way, it was sooo frustrating. It had been Jessica's most overt overture yet, and her most stunning, steaming failure.

Her pale little hand flew in her clinging blue shorts now, her other hand crushing her pert little boobs under the skin-tight yellow top that completed her re-donned volleyball uniform. She was sooo in love with Andie, just *had* to get the girl to love her back. The tension and frustration was too much, too many nights spent exactly like this – all by herself with just her hands and fingers and vibrators and dildos and dirty DVDs and books to keep her lonely, lustful company.

She yanked her hand out of her shorts and grabbed onto the elasticated waistband with both hands, arched her bum off the bed, and shoved the sweaty pair of shorts down. She rolled her sweaty top up with equal angry resolve, so that her pussy and boobs were bare, coursing with heat and feeling. She then plunged two fingers into her shaved, sodden slit and urgently pumped, gripping and groping her breasts, pulling on the jutting pink tips. Jessica savagely fucked and felt herself up, furiously focusing on Andie, her wet dreamgirl whom she didn't seem to have a hope of ever capturing for herself.

Jessica didn't even know for sure if Andie liked other girls the way she liked other girls. She only knew that Andie didn't have a boyfriend, that she socialised with a number of other girls. Maybe it wasn't personal, just preferential. Still, Jessica bit her lip and blinked tears out of her eyes, pushing her pelvis up to meet her pistoning fingers, squeezing her left breast so hard the nipple distended obscenely. All she knew for sure was that Andie barely knew she was alive. And that was crushing enough for any 18-year-old girl in love.

'I'll get you yet – bitch!' Jessica snarled, furious at her own awkwardness that made meaningful, direct, and unequivocal flirtation with Andie almost impossible. If she couldn't even talk to the girl, find out her feelings for real, what chance did she have of ever fucking her?

Jessica jerked her breast back to her mouth, but she couldn't reach the straining nipple with her outstretched tongue. So she fiercely pinched the nipple, and added another driving finger to her molten pussy and her thumb to her swelled-up clit. She pounded into herself fast and frantic, pinched her nipple to popping, her curvy little body dewed with perspiration and her violet eyes fixed with purpose. And as brutal orgasm broke inside her burning body, churned through her in shuddering, searing waves, the girl's ferociously concentrated expression suddenly smoothed and shone on her pretty face. As she, at last, figured out how she could, for sure, capture Andie all for herself.

Jessica had to work a second part-time job for a number of months, and clean out her college fund savings, before she could raise enough capital. And even then the president of The Companion Company was sceptical. It was his corporate and legal duty to try to gently dissuade infatuated teenagers from wasting their money on what might just be a passing phase. But Jessica was of age, and determined, so she eventually got exactly what she wanted, custom-built.

The girl was so nervous and excited when the delivery man finally brought the huge box up to her bedroom that she almost peed her panties. She was wearing her best dress and high heels, her dark hair done up with strands dangling down in coils, eyes shadowed, and lips glossed and cheeks powdered. The delivery man had barely left her perfumed room, when Jessica slammed the door in her parents' disapproving faces, pried the upright cardboard container open, and pulled the Styrofoam stabilisers and protective plastic wrapping off the figure inside.

'H-hello … A-Andie,' she stammered, pulling on one of the figure's fingers.

The girl's green eyes lit up, and her plush lips formed a smile. 'Hello, Jessica,' she responded warmly.

Jessica giddily clutched her hands together, her heart racing, her bare arms and legs shaking. Andie was beautiful, her smooth, bronze skin and silky, blonde hair gleaming under the muted bedroom lights, her flat stomach and lush breasts with darker brown nipples moving gently up and down, her blonde-furred pussy on full, delicious display. They were together, alone, in Jessica's bedroom. Soft music played in the background.

'W-won't you sit down?' Jessica stuttered.

She stumbled backwards and plopped down on the edge of her bed, showing what she meant. She realised now that she was overdressed for the awesome occasion, overscented and over-made-up, given Andie's stark, stunning nudity right out of the box. But she *had* so wanted to make a good first impression.

Andie said, 'OK,' and walked over to the bed and sat down next to Jessica.

The girl's bared shoulder touched Jessica's. Jessica flinched and flushed with joy at the warm, soft feel.

'I-I've wanted to … get to know you so much better, for s-such a long time,' Jessica spluttered, gazing at Andie's lovely, oval face, her full, pointed breasts, her slender, shapely legs with the tuft of fur in between.

Jessica swallowed hard and boldly reached out her right hand, slid the trembling, damp hand onto Andie's left thigh. 'Ooooh!' she gasped, grasping the hot, taut, brown flesh.

Andie smiled and blinked.

Jessica rubbed Andie's thigh, her own thighs under the short hem of her red dress shimmering with heat, her pussy at the apex brimming with emotion. 'I-I don't want to rush you … Andie,' Jessica mumbled, looking up into the girl's eyes. 'But … I've wanted to do this – with you – for so long.'

Andie's full lips moved. 'Whatever you'd like to do, Jessica.'

Jessica pulled her hand up Andie's thigh, her fingers brushing fur as they dragged by. Then she slid her hand around onto the small of Andie's curved back, reached out with her other quivering hand, and hooked it onto Andie's right shoulder. She turned the girl slightly to face her more fully, then moved her head forward, slowly, excruciatingly, her eyes hooding and glazing as her trembling lips parted. Andie met her halfway. Their open mouths pressed together.

Jessica shivered with delight, her face and body flaming. Andie's lips were ever so soft and responsive, moving against Jessica's. She fully closed her eyes and revelled in the overwhelming sensualness of it all, her left hand gliding down Andie's shoulder to cup her breast.

'Mmmm!' Jessica breathed softly in Andie's mouth, squeezing the heavy, heated flesh of Andie's breast.

She could hardly believe it was actually happening. But it *was* happening. Andie's hand reached up and closed over Jessica's breast, and the sexually electrified girl cried out with passion.

Jessica just couldn't control herself after that. She pushed Andie down on the bed and grabbed onto both of the girl's breasts, smothering Andie's mouth with her own. She swirled her tongue all around Andie's lips, darted her tongue into Andie's mouth, kneading the girl's boobs. Andie's tongue instantly darted out and entwined with Jessica's, pink and wet and alive. Jessica sucked on Andie's tongue, Andie sucked on Jessica's tongue.

Jessica kissed her way down Andie's strong chin and long, slender neck, all over Andie's gently rising and falling chest. Then she squeezed the girl's breasts even tighter in her gripping hands, pushed them together, and poured her brazen lips over one of Andie's burnt-sugar nipple and sucked, before jumping her head over and excitedly sucking on Andie's other nipple. They were thick and rubbery, tasted delicious. Jessica could actually, thrillingly feel them swell in her mouth as she tugged on them.

It was everything she'd fantasised and masturbated over and more, even better. And she wanted more – she wanted it all, now.

She sucked on Andie's breasts for a minute or so, then twirled her tongue all around the girl's glistening, pebbled areolas, flogged the fully erect nipples and bit into them. And then Jessica released Andie's luscious breasts, hands, and mouth and slid the girl up higher on the bed, slid her hands down lower on the girl's contours. She kissed and licked Andie's softly undulating stomach, tongued inside Andie's cute little belly button, kissed her way in between the girl's parted legs.

Jessica gripped Andie's flared hips and stared into the girl's downy sex. She could see through the blonde fur the tan, wrinkly lips of Andie's slit. Jessica gulped and dove her face into Andie's pussy.

It was wanton, wild, wonderful – finally she was getting intimate with the girl she'd been lusting after for so long. Jessica dug her eager tongue into Andie's slit and writhed it around inside of the girl, tasting the heat and, yes, moisture. She slid her hands back up and grasped Andie's breasts again, squeezing the exquisite pair once more, as she bobbed her head back and forth, licking Andie's delightful pussy.

Jessica lapped Andie's slit from deep in between the girl's legs to the top of the girl's fur, her tongue slathering pubes and flaps and upraised pink button with excited stroke after stroke. She pinched and rolled Andie's rigid nipples between her fingers, lustily licking the girl's pussy. Until she remembered lovemaking was something to be shared, no matter how much one party owed to the other.

Jessica jerked her head up and smacked her lips, focused her blurry eyes. Andie was smiling at her. She let go of the girl's breasts and squirmed off the bed. Jumping to her feet, she shed her satin dress, stripped off her lace bra and panties, and kicked off her red leather high heels.

She stepped naked out of the fallen garments. Her body glowed, the stiffened tips of her breasts throbbing, her soaking pussy beating with wicked arousal. Jessica looked down at Andie's beautiful, laid-out, waiting body, the girl's breasts and pussy shining with her own saliva. And then she pounced.

Jessica landed on all fours over the top of Andie on the bed. She kissed her on the lips, then quickly spun around so that she was facing Andie's pussy, and Andie was facing her pussy. She grasped the girl's lean thighs and dipped her head down and hissed, 'Lick my pussy, Andie! Please lick my pussy!'

Her wish was Andie's command – literally. The girl

reached up, gripped Jessica's bubble butt cheeks, and lifted her head in between Jessica's bent legs to plunge her tongue into Jessica's pussy.

'Ohmigod! Yes!' Jessica shrieked, Andie's long, full-bodied tongue hitting home.

Andie's tongue squirmed strongly around inside Jessica's pussy, juicing the gasping girl with even more fervour. Jessica pumped her pelvis, humping her pussy up and down on Andie's tongue, fucking herself on the outrageously extended appendage. Until Andie pulled her tongue out and applied it to Jessica's entire dazzled slit, in long, hard, dragging, wet strokes.

'Yes! Yes!' Jessica wailed, undulating against that widened, washing tongue. She dropped her dizzied head down into Andie's pussy and started licking her again with equal vigour.

Andie's pussy brimmed with moisture, just like her own. Jessica scooped the tangy flavoured juices out of Andie's slit with her tongue just like Andie was doing to her. It was all so sensational, so staggeringly, erotically realistic.

Jessica's fingernails bit into Andie's taut thighs as she bobbed her head urgently in between, slurping frantically up and down Andie's pussy. She could feel the orgasm building and building up in her own pussy, on the end of Andie's stroking tongue, ready to burst into ecstasy.

Andie lapped Jessica from puffed-up clit all the way to tingling bumhole, around the world and out of this world. Over and over and over, rhythmically and relentlessly. Jessica blazed with the heated striping, buttocks quivering out of control in Andie's gripping hands, as the girl lashed her clit one time too incredibly many. She raised her head up from Andie's sodden pussy and shuddered repeatedly, her eyes clamping shut and mouth wrenching open in a silent scream. Orgasm engulfed her entirely in scorching, head-spinning wave after wave.

They lay together under the covers afterwards, Jessica hugging Andie's hot, nude body tight to her own naked, glowing body. Andie's arms were around Jessica and her head rested on the girl's shoulder. 'We'll be together for ever,' Jessica cooed, stroking Andie's blonde hair and bronze shoulder. 'I don't need anyone –'

The door to her bedroom suddenly popped open. Andie stood in the doorway – Andie Perkins, Jessica's classmate.

'Your mother said … I could … find you here,' the beautiful, honey-blonde, sunkissed girl said. Her widened green eyes looked from Jessica's startled face to the companion's serene face, lingered on the companion's familiar features.

'I'm, uh, flattered … I guess,' Andie said, slowly walking into the room and up to Jessica's bed, staring at her exact double.

Jessica bit her lip and said nothing, anxiously looking up at her inspiration.

Andie sat down on the side of the bed, next to the companion. 'I, um, *thought* you had … feelings for me,' she said, speaking to Jessica but gazing at Jessica's companion. 'But I didn't realise they ran *this* deep.' She pulled the bedcovers back to reveal the companion's bare torso, the exact replica of her own lush breasts.

'I-I didn't th-think you n-noticed,' Jessica stammered, ashamed, yet with a renewed warmth spreading inside her body, with the real Andie so close.

Andie touched the companion's shoulder, caressed the smooth, skin-like surface with her fingertips. She caught her breath when the companion stirred and smiled at her.

Andie tore her eyes away from her double and looked

at Jessica. She smiled, herself, reached over and cupped Jessica's chin, stroked the girl's electrified skin. 'Jessica,' she breathed through her plush pink lips, 'do you think you ... I –'

'Yes, Andie! Yes!' Jessica squealed, her nipples popped and pussy surging with heat and moisture. In a funny, wacky, wonderful way it was all working out for her, after all – her passion for Andie fully exposed, she and Andie together at last.

'Do you think ... I'd be able to borrow Andie?' her classmate asked, gazing lustfully at her naked, gorgeous duplicate.

Shattering Jessica's dreams yet again.

She's Not There
by Shea Lancaster

Sometimes, people get under your skin. It's a fact of life. It may be that you are on a train and the passenger opposite you sniffs all the way through your journey. It may be that someone you work with tells really lousy jokes and yet you feel forced to laugh. But, ever so occasionally, along comes the type of person whom you can go for years without seeing, but who stays at the forefront of your memory, waiting for the opportunity to emerge and torment you once more.

For me, that latter itch was my experience. It began as a fucked-up roller coaster of an affair. Both hurting, we were flung together at a time when it only took one common element to bind us. We grasped that equal footing and fled with it until we ran out of energy and its power was not sufficient to sustain us any longer. I do not recall how it truly ended; it was as though, on that final day, as we parted we knew we would never see each other again.

Yet I would be lying to myself if I said I never thought of her. She occupies the drowsy final thoughts of consciousness before sleep swallows me. Her skin is the skin I feel in my mind as my fingers push to release my frustration. At the peak of my raw, primal convulsing, her nipple is the nipple the teeth of my imagination clenches.

And yet, as I fall asleep, her arms are not the arms to envelop me. Her place in my mind is that of my ultimate escape. The nights spent with her in my mind's eye are my forbidden secret. Forcing her into me is my shameful fantasy; it dips and rises in its frequency over the years but never leaves me completely.

It sits there at present, unveiling itself like a vampire at night, to have disappeared by dawn. It manifests itself as her figure, her face, her fingers, her shoulders. The location is always the same. The one room she occupies is a cavern of possibility and fantasy. In my vision we are in her room, on her couch, discussing the one thing that, in its gossamer form, joined us in the very beginning and held us fast. Music. More than two years' worth of beloved song being discussed, played, considered, concurred with, and dismissed. There is wine, but I do not drink it. To do so would be a betrayal. Instead, I have a Coke, or a tea, or even water. To imagine myself as sober would be a scenario not impossible to believe, but I know there would be a joint in my hand, then in her hand, as it passes between us. The conversation becomes less stilted but also less coherent. And I am less self-conscious and she is quieter.

I'd like to think my resolve would hold out for longer but it can't. I have no control over this any more. I agonise over the crucial moment of my possession of her. I do not know if it is a clichéd brush of hair over her forehead, or a touching of her hand, or even a predatory kissing of her neck, unexpected, as she inspects another song. Whatever the catalyst, the result is the same, as she reciprocates, tentatively at first. We both know we cannot be in this enclosed space without the hunger I have for her manifesting itself, and yet she graciously pantomimes surprise and even reluctance. Her lips are parted and she pulls away from me just enough to give me the pleasure of making that first contact. I'm the one who moves forward, who throws everything aside, who can think of nothing but devouring her. The kisses are respectfully chaste to begin with, but soon we abandon the pretence and her tongue is as exploratory as mine, and she does not move my hands as they spread over her back, then down to her arse, the tops of her legs, and back up to her waist.

The taste of her is heartbreakingly familiar; the ironic perfume she wears declares I should use caution but instead it makes me want her more. This is not some old, traditional sexual need. It is not an attraction coming to a head. It's an urge I cannot control. It is years of thinking about her, imagining her, talking to her, hearing her answer, finding her voice in every song. Time almost literally stands still and the universe could implode and I would be utterly ignorant.

We are on her bed and I lift her T-shirt to reveal the strappy black undershirt she wears. The swirl of her tattoo has its unwavering hypnotic command as its familiarity makes me groan. I lick her neck, from her ear to her shoulder, tracing the ink with my tongue and turning her around to devour the image. We kneel on the bed like this, my hands holding her to me as her back presses against my breasts; she lets me lick her tattoo until not an inch remains untasted and my hands drift from her waist to her breasts. I don't cup them gently but rather grab them, holding them in the palm of my hands, pinching them to snap to attention her nipples. They comply and I rub them slowly, continuing to lick her neck, biting her shoulders and whispering to her. I remind her of the first time we met. I do not know if she remembers, or if she pretends not to recall. I tell her what I could see as I undressed her, as she shimmied up the bed towards the pillows. I whisper to her that, as though it was seconds ago, I remember peeling off her pants to see her cunt glistening with its wetness. I tell her that I don't forget it. And I tell her I want to make her as wet as that all over again.

I am not sure of her response. In my fantasy I want her to moan for me, to grasp my hands with her own and force me to clench her breasts even harder. I want her to press her back into me, to throw back her neck so that it rests on my shoulders in utter submission. This would be my invitation to possess her. And I would waste no time in it. Now she lies on her back and lets me wrench off her jeans, and her slender legs wrap around my waist and pull me into her. I am unhappy about the amount of control she has and I grab her hands and hold them over her head; in doing so my face meets hers and it is all I can do to hold her gaze, to look straight into her eyes, to inspect her without words, before the need to kiss her succeeds my wish to be impassive and belligerent. The softness of the way I kiss her belies the cold exterior I am desperate to maintain. I cannot help but put aside my aggression for just a few moments as she responds by tightening her grip with her legs and pulling me into her. I free her arms, trusting her not to misbehave, and she welcomes the flash of freedom, but chooses to stay, wrapping her arms around my neck and twining my hair around her fingers. She kisses me with the softness of a lover and I reciprocate, and our tongues speak their wordless musings to each other and we are not privy to their conversation. I lick her lips, and she bites me softly in return, and I do not know when I started to move against her but her hips are locked to mine and she is giving herself to me and I am taking what she offers.

I break away to pull at the straps of her top; instead of

lifting the top over her head I pull it down, so it sits at her waist and reveals her breasts. She is silent, and I have no words in return, and she holds my head as I gaze at her breasts. I rub my thumb lightly on her nipple and she shifts a little with a sensitive shudder. I am amazed at how I can be hypnotized by something so small but her nipple demands to be given attention and I oblige. I kiss it lightly before parting my lips and savouring the feel of my tongue coming into contact with her breast. I begin to lick at the nipple like a kitten licks at milk before I cannot hold out any longer and instead take her whole breast in my mouth and suck on her nipple as though it is giving me life. This is what I have wanted. This is what I have dreamt about. This is what has caused me to give myself the biggest orgasms of my life. The dream of her breasts is finally once more a reality and I proceed to claim her, alternating from one nipple to the other, covering her chest in my saliva and licking it back again, bringing into my mouth and swallowing with it the scent of her skin, the taste of her freckles, the flavour of her. I am almost delirious with desire and bite her breast, sucking hard just outside the areola, causing her to scream in pain. I clamp my hand over her mouth to quieten her and continue to bite, sometimes softly, but mostly with grim power and purpose. Her chest is covered with red marks but I am not satisfied. I rip off the undershirt, which is now impeding me, and she lies on her back with only her black knickers on. I leave them there, as one leaves a gift still wrapped, staring at it, wanting to open it, but relishing the thrill of its unattainability.

She begins to struggle and I hold her down, but she is strong. She forgets, however, that my weight is between her legs and I hold her down on the bed by my hips, and she grimaces in pain as the belt from my jeans pinches her naked skin. I do not wish to submit to her, but rather crave the feeling of my skin on hers. For that reason I sit up and place my hand on her chest slowly, to wordlessly instruct her to remain exactly where she is. I make her watch me as I unbuckle my jeans and she instinctively lifts a hand to help me. I allow her to wrench open the clasp of the belt and to unbutton my jeans and I slide them off my legs and throw them onto the couch. I unbutton my shirt and leave it on, but open, to reveal my bra, and now I am in my underwear, between her legs, and I can feel her skin against mine, and the strong muscles of her thighs gripping me once more. She feels as though she wants me, the way she moves her body, the way her nipples remain stiff and beckoning, the way the heat from between her legs seeps through my own pants and warms me. There remains just one way to gauge her want.

My fingers find the seam of her pants and I fix my eyes onto hers once more as I peel off the last vestige of her modesty. She is neatly shaven, the red-blonde hairs short and soft. My eyes flick away from hers as I let them wander down, past her taut and bruised nipples, past her bitten stomach, down to her cunt. I throw the pants away and grab her thighs, forcing them apart so I can regard her at my leisure. And a surge of triumphant power rushes through me as I see what I have waited literally years to see.

She is dripping wet. I can smell her now, like a beast unleashed, and her musky spice drifts over me, causing me to cry out, and her pink, wet pussy is soaking the covers underneath her. She is all mine. She is wet for me. The chasm between her legs is displayed for my pleasure and I close my eyes and breathe in deeply, still prising her legs apart. I cry in frustration because I want to own this woman in every way I can, only the idea of owning her is insufficient. I want to claim her, to hold her, to eat her, to bite her, to grab her, to fuck her, to pin her down, to tear into her skin, to rip her apart. And I waste no time. She tries to sit up but I push her down again with my left hand, cupping her throat, applying enough pressure for her to gurgle in shock and submit. She grabs my hair and pulls me into her face as she bites my throat like a lioness, licking me to my ear, where she speaks to me for the first time in what feels like hours.

'I knew you'd be back,' she snarls at me. She does not need to elaborate. She knows that her hypnotic cunt has teased me since the very first day I saw it. But I cannot allow her to exert her control over me without a fight, and in response I keep my left hand on her throat but my right hand I introduce to her steaming hot pussy, as I plunge not one, not two, but three fingers inside her. They slide into her hotness without a murmur of complaint; instead she shouts in relief as I claim her with my hand, soaking my fingers. I search for her G-spot and fuck it furiously, pushing myself into her, giving her every ounce of frustration I have felt whilst being apart from her. I make her experience my desire for her, so there can be no doubt, and as I massage her from the inside I communicate with my fingers how much I have wanted her. She closes her eyes and submits to me easily, and I relish her surrender and continue to fuck her, faster and harder, biting her nipples and keeping my hand on her throat. Three fingers are not enough for her and I slide in another, before curling my thumb into my palm and introducing my fist.

She gasps and her eyes flash open and she lifts her neck from the pillow, looking at me, her mouth open in rapture, watching me as I force my fist inside her; my hand disappears and I am literally up to my wrist in her cunt. This isn't the first time I have filled her but she remains as tight she was an age hence, and my hand is being clamped by her as though in a vice. I am still for a moment, allowing her to adapt to the force with which I have taken her, and slowly I feel the muscles inside start to relax as she sinks into the pillows, groaning, and opens up to me. I can reach up and touch her cervix, and she flinches at the sensitive invasion. But I don't stop; instead I stroke her from the inside, beckoning her to me, and she opens her legs even wider, pushing me into her more deeply.

'Remember this?' I murmur, and she nods between gasps.

'Who owns this cunt?' I ask her. She shakes her head and bites her lip.

'Who owns this cunt?' I repeat the question, watching her wrestle with herself. She writhes as if to fight me, but the ever-relaxing muscles of her red hot pussy belie her defensiveness.

I ask her one more time.

'Who owns this cunt?'

'You!' she screams. 'You always fucking owned it. You fucking bitch!'

This is what I wanted to hear. This is what I have spent hours imagining her saying to me. I love to hear her guttural cries, her frustrated yelling, her fucking filthy, hard-headed determination expressed in anger like this. I want to claim her as my own but at the same time fuck her to within an inch of her life and leave her begging for more. I start to withdraw my hand but she stops me. It confirms what I knew about her, that she wants me like I want her. She hasn't finished yet but I'm not complaining, for I am far from finishing with her. I continue to fuck her deeply, and she moves with me in her rhythm, muttering unintelligibly to herself, opening herself to me both physically and emotionally, and I take my opportunity and seize her with my tongue.

My wetness against hers is a surprise and she opens her eyes once more, crying out to see me adore her clit. She is still soaking wet and I collect every drop of her, swallowing over and over, relishing her familiar taste. Her clit is hard under the touch of my tongue and I start to concentrate on making it behave the way I want it to. As I am pushing her from the inside I am sucking on her clit, and the hand I had around her throat moves down to her nipples and back again. She bucks against me, harder and harder, and cries out in what seems like pain, but rather than stop, concerned, I carry on, invigorated, pummelling her hole and sucking on her clit to force her to climax for me. She flings her hands onto my back and scrapes her nails across my skin, leaving me flooded with a euphoria that makes me shout in untold agonising bliss. I can feel the gouges she has carved into my back, the icy air stinging my skin, proving she has made me bleed in her frenzy. But I know she's not finished yet, and she continues to rub against me, now pressing my head into her even more, and she rubs, faster and faster, and I am still controlling her, fisting her heavenly Utopia, whilst flicking my tongue over and over her clit until finally, with a huge scream, she holds me tight against her and floods me. I feel her wetness explode over my face and drench the sheets and she contracts from within, over and over, tightening on my wrist and forcing my fingers to fold in on themselves whilst I still occupy her.

All manner of unintelligible obscenities burst from her lips as she curses me and adores me in one breath. I slowly retract my hand from her and depart, leaving her empty, but whole. She cannot open her eyes to look at

49

me; she lies on the sodden bed, still writhing, still twitching, and there are tears of determined agony running down the sides of her eyes and into her hair. I am exhausted and utterly in awe of the flood that erupted in my face. I go to lick her dry but she cannot cope with me touching her, and instead I kiss her thighs and suck on them gently while she mutters to herself and falls into exhausted half-consciousness.

With that image, I flash back into the solitude of my bed, the reality of my longing encapsulated in my own powerful orgasm. Once it subsides, and my heartbeat struggles to maintain rhythm, I lie alone, empty and desolate, praying that this has been an exorcism on my part; a ridding of the itch of her that drives me insane.

But I am not a fool. It remains there still, under my skin, until next time.

Dirty Little Secret
by Valerie Grey

Elli looked so fucking sexy as she emerged, cautiously, from the side of the house. She was wearing the little black skirt I'd bought her; it barely covered her pussy and ass. She had on a red halter top, and her short, brown hair was pinned up so that her bangs hung around her face. I liked that she had put on soft pink lipstick and done her nails the same colour. She walked quickly over to the car and jumped into the passenger seat.

'I'm pretty sure he didn't see me,' she said, breathless.

'Good,' I said.

I put the car in gear, backed out of the driveway, and pulled away.

'You look pretty,' I told her.

Her eyes lit up; they looked very clear and bright when we drove under a streetlamp. Her voice was awkward. 'Thanks. You too.' She was a bit nervous.

There was no way her husband would have approved of her outfit; sneaking her out of the house was the only way to complete our little mission. She had asked for the skirt for her birthday. She turned 21 and wanted to be bold. It was our "secret gift". At the party, yesterday, I'd given her a pink unicorn doll, my "not secret gift". She had pretended to like it.

'The movie starts at eight,' I said. 'So hopefully he's

asleep before we get home. Otherwise, sneaking you back in might be tricky.'

'Yeah. I *don't* want to get caught.'

When she had asked for the skirt, she'd also asked for another "secret gift". She wanted me to take her out on a date. I was, needless to say, surprised. She said a "sister date" when I'd asked her what she meant.

I wasn't sure what a "sister date" was exactly. I assumed she just meant a friendly night out at the movies. And yet, she knew I was a lesbian. I hadn't pressed the issue. It was her birthday, and I'd take her out on a date and make it the best date I possibly could. If it meant anything more to her, well, we would find out.

I looked down at Elli's legs, sticking out from the bottom of the skirt. She was a bit paler than me, with light freckles. Her left knee had a bright red bruise, I guess from soccer practice. She was younger than me by three years, married at 19. I couldn't help thinking the black satin fabric lying across her thighs was the most sexy sight ever.

She noticed my wanton, wandering eyes. 'Watch the road,' she said, smiling.

We arrived at the theatre. I parked the car and got out. Elli waited in her seat, smiling at me.

'You'll open my door for me, right?' she said.

This was her birthday gift. I wanted her to be happy. I went around to her side and opened her door for her. She took my hand as she got out and leant into me. She seemed very nervous.

'Would you hold my hand?' she asked.

I was wearing a short red dress with heels. I was a few inches taller than her, and slender. She had an athletic build and moved very gracefully. I grasped her hand, and we walked together up to the theatre.

I am quite sure we looked amazing.

After we were through the door, Elli broke away to go get some candy.

I caught a guy staring at her as she walked away. He noticed me, and looked away embarrassed.

I said, jokingly, 'You can look, but don't touch,' thinking my double meaning made me clever.

Her skirt fit her perfectly. I hadn't really seen her clearly in the dim light outside, and I hadn't actually seen her from behind until now. When she got to the counter, she squatted down to pick out some candy. Her ass and legs looked amazing.

We found seats in the auditorium. Elli insisted that we sit way in back, in a corner. The armrests were the type you could fold up, so she pulled up the one between us and leant into me. Yes, doctor, it was obvious she was taking this date thing a bit too seriously, and I felt a little awkward. However, I didn't want to push her away, and to be quite honest, I liked that she was being so affectionate. Her curled up against me felt nice. I decided she hadn't crossed any lines yet. I put my arm around her and pulled her close.

The movie started. It was one of Woody Allen's offerings, full of neurotic wit and literary references I knew Elli probably did not comprehend.

She handed me the box of candy and whispered, '*Feed me.*'

'What?'

'Take one and put it into my mouth.'

'Elli, that is a little weird.'

'*Please.*'

The theatre was dark, and I could only see her silhouette. I felt her push closer to me. I took out a piece of candy and put it into her mouth. She wrapped her mouth around my fingers and sucked gently, swallowing the candy down.

'*Elli!*' I whispered. That was loud enough to be heard. I certainly didn't want anyone to notice what was going on. I went on whispering. 'Elli. That's very weird.'

She drew away from me.

'Look,' I went on, 'did you intend for this to be a romantic date?' She didn't answer right away. I knew exactly what she was thinking. I mean, it was obvious what was going on. I couldn't quite believe it, but there was no way to pretend it wasn't happening.

I knew she was afraid to say yes. If she did I might freak out, and that would end everything.

But I knew she wouldn't say no.

'Yes, a little bit,' she whispered.

She sat still; tense, waiting for my response.

It is amazing how fast you can make a life-changing decision. My impulse was to give her some speech about how I loved her, but that this was inappropriate. She was so soft, and so pretty. Even in the dim light, her slight, athletic figure looked amazing. I could see her hair silhouetted around her face.

The scene on the movie screen changed, lighting her up. Her green eyes stared at me. She sucked on her lower lip nervously.

I wanted her so much.

I put my arm back around her and pulled her close again. I whispered in her ear, 'I love you Elli, very much.' Then I took another piece of candy and put it into her mouth.

She suckled gently on my fingers. Her tongue and lips were so soft and wet. I thought about how they would feel later, against me, sucking and licking. I felt a thrill pass through me.

I *knew* I was going to fuck this sweet, beautiful girl.

We didn't finish the movie. I made her walk in front of me through the lobby. I wanted to see her nice, round ass again.

'How long have you felt this way?' I asked as we drove home.

'A while. Since we went to that summer dance.'

'And you waited until now?'

'Well, I mean, I assumed you would be horrified. But I kept wanting you so bad, and I had to try something.'

She was sitting up stiff, obviously very nervous. She gave me a sheepish look. I reached over and stroked her body.

'Relax, sweetie,' I said, 'I'm very happy you did. I mean, yeah, I'm a little freaked out, but this is going to be very good.'

We got to a stop sign and I leant over and kissed her mouth. She was surprised, but parted her lips and leant into me, kissing me back passionately.

'Do you know much about sex with another woman?'

'I kissed a girl once,' she confessed, 'but we didn't do anything.'

'Have you ever masturbated thinking of another woman?'

'*No!*' she said.

'You can tell me the truth.'

I hoped she'd say she masturbated thinking about me. She admitted, 'Yeah, I have.'

'Have you ever had an orgasm thinking about other women?' I asked.

Softly: 'I don't think so.'

Amused: 'Trust me, *you'd know.*'

'Guess I would, huh?'

'So, here is what we do,' I went on, 'when we get

home you're going to sneak me into your room and lock the door. We'll start just kissing. Will that be fine?'

She nodded. 'Yes.'

'So, we can just kiss if you want. But I'm going to want to do more. So, after a while, I'll start doing things to your body, with my mouth and stuff. It'll feel really good.'

'Yeah.'

'Don't be nervous. You should just relax and let it feel good. It might take a while, but don't worry about me.'

'You don't want me to do anything to you?'

I smiled. 'I want you to do *lots* of things to me, sweetie, but first we take care of you. After a while, it will start feeling really, intensely good. Just relax. Pretty soon you'll have an orgasm. And then you'll understand everything.'

'Then I get to do you?' she said.

'Yeah. Then you get to do me.'

When we got home, her husband was already in bed and sleeping like the dead, like he always did after drinking beer and vodka. It was easy to sneak Elli back into the house. She took me with her, and we went down into the basement. She hugged me and we kissed deeply. She pressed her tongue into my mouth, and sucked in my breath. I rubbed her ass, pulling her skirt up and feeling her soft panties. I turned her around and pushed her down on the bed. I pulled her skirt up, then pulled her panties up into the crack of her ass, and kissed her butt cheeks. She moaned softly.

I wanted to take her badly. I wanted to pull her panties aside, eat her pussy and ream her asshole, but I stopped myself and my wanting tongue. She was such a kind, sweet girl, and I didn't think her first time should be wild or kinky. I turned her back around and kissed her again.

She lay back on the bed passively, and looked up at me licking her lips. She reached up, slowly, and rubbed my chest. I felt her fingers brush against my nipples. She kept rubbing, and watching the look of pleasure on my face.

'That feels nice,' I said, as I pulled the top of my dress down. 'You can suck on them, if you want.'

She sat up and helped me take off my bra.

We kissed deeply again, then she took my nipple into her mouth and nibbled gently. I ran my fingers through her hair, and stroked her back. Her mouth felt great on my tits, and I was going crazy with desire. I almost pushed her down again, but I held back. I wanted to take my time, and make this wonderful for her.

I helped her pull her top off, and did the same to her. Her chest was small, A-cups, and her nipples were soft, pink, and slightly dimpled.

She reached up my dress, rubbing her fingers slowly up my leg toward my pussy. She watched me, seeing if I'd stop her.

I spread my legs, just enough so she could reach. She gently stroked my soft panties, rubbing her finger up and down over my cunt. I felt a shock of pleasure pass through me.

'Elli, that feels really great, but I want to do you first.'

She gave me a devious look and said, 'Plans can change. Can I eat it?'

She looked so pretty and eager. I couldn't say no.

'If you want,' I said.

'I just lick, right?'

'And suck too. But yeah, it isn't difficult.'

She pulled my panties down and spread my legs and gave my pussy a long, slow, tentative tongue-fuck.

'That is really good,' I told her.

I pulled the hem of my dress up higher, so I could see

her face. She looked up at me passionately, and kissed my clit, sucking gently on it. I felt tingles of pleasure spread up through my body.

I let out a long, deep moan.

'Should I stick my fingers in?'

'Please yes,' I went, 'two would be peachy keen.'

She rubbed two of her fingers up and down my pussy, getting them moist, then slowly pushed them into my hole, pulling them in and out slowly.

She continued to suck on my clit. I was in ecstasy.

'Will you please do that a little faster, please?'

I looked down at her pretty face with her mouth wrapped around my cunt, and I couldn't hold back. A wave of ecstasy passed over my body like syrup over pancakes. I could feel my hips bucking up. Elli grabbed me tight around the thighs to keep her face planted to my pussy. I shook my head back and forth, as several more waves passed over me.

I couldn't think. It was almost too much.

I could see her there, still holding on and licking. I would have begged her to stop, it was just too intense, but I couldn't form words.

I came again, gasping for air like a goldfish deprived of water.

I gently push her head back from my cunt.

She sat back, surprised at the intensity of my orgasm.

'Please kiss me, please,' I said.

We embraced, and kissed deeply.

'Was it good?' she asked.

'You're kidding, right?' I had to catch my breath again. 'That was the most amazing fucking thing.'

I had to rest. I couldn't move in any coordinated way. My body still tingled, and I gasped a few times as my muscles tightened up, as if my orgasm wasn't entirely finished.

She rubbed my pussy some more, but she was too eager. I said, 'Please, *gently,* sweetie.'

We kept kissing, and gradually I calmed down.

'It is your turn now,' I said.

She went to pull her panties down and I stopped her.

'Leave them on for a bit; they're so soft and pretty.'

I pushed her skirt up and wrapped my mouth around her clit, through the sheer fabric. She let out a light, gentle, little moan.

I sucked a bit harder, and pushed her panties a bit into her hole with my thumb.

'That feels nice,' she said with her mouth slightly parted. I pulled her panties off and pushed her skirt up around her tummy. Her pussy was thin and delicately shaped. It was light pink, with just a hint of brown hair surrounding it. I spread it open, and ran my tongue gently up from her hole to her clit.

She squirmed a bit and tensed.

I said, 'Relax. You don't have to do anything but lay back and feel good.'

I licked around her hole until she started to get very wet, then plunged into her, kind of scooping up a bit of her juices on my tongue. I licked up to her clit, then pulled away slowly and let a thin strand of pussy juice stretch between my tongue and her pussy.

She said, 'I've never been so wet.'

'You taste good.'

I slipped a finger in.

Her eyes were closed. She would briefly open them, every few seconds, and look down at me devouring her, then close them again with a look of rapture on her face.

I started fingering and licking her with a rhythmic motion. I felt her trying to relax, like I told her, but I could tell it was getting close. She kept tensing up, and writhing a bit, before relaxing again.

Her breathing got very heavy, and she let out a long, deep, soothing moan. I felt her whole body tighten up.

'*Is this it*?' she cried.

She looked at me intensely, seemed to relax for a second; it slammed her back into the bed. I kept sucking on her clit, just as she'd done for me, and let the waves pass over her. It seemed to last for ever. She laughed, still panting, and got the biggest grin on her face I've ever seen on anyone.

She said, 'Is it *always* like *that*?'

I got up and lay next to her, putting my arms around her and kissing her face and eyes. 'Yes, my sweet Elli, it is *always* like that.'

'Can we do it again?'

'Yeah. Now?'

'*Can we*?'

And so we did, several times each. The later orgasms, of course, were not as intense; her final one only getting a long, gentle moan from her.

She curled up next to me. We were both too tired to even really kiss any more, only managing to brush our fumbling lips against each other.

I whispered into her ear, 'That was the best date I've ever had.'

'*Sister*,' she said.

Of course there were problems: I was her husband's sister. I lived in the same house, but it later became easy for us to keep our lust, our love, secret, because her husband, my dolt brother, never suspected a fucking thing. I had to see her and not touch her, I had to keep my mouth shut and not say lewd suggestive things when he was around. It was the dirty little secret in the family.

Sugar, Sugar
by Heidi Champa

I knew I could get a burger anywhere. Hell, there was a fast food joint on nearly every corner in town. Sometimes more than one, fighting it out for supremacy. That didn't even take into account all the diners, dives and bars that filled the streets near where I lived. Instead, I chose to drive 30 miles out of my way and out of town to the refurbished and redesigned drive-in that dripped with so much nostalgia, I was always expecting for the cast of *Happy Days* to be waiting there for me. I would drive my restored wood-panelled station wagon all that way there, both for the great food and the kitsch factor I just couldn't get anywhere else.

All the waitresses dressed in pitch-perfect Fifties style, with their own personal touches, of course. I still have no idea how the tall redhead got all those locks into a beehive, but I appreciated the effort all the same. What could I say? I was a sucker for that kind of thing. If I could have crammed all of the drive-in into my apartment, I would have. That was why I spent so much time there. Well, that was the only reason at first. Then, I met Zarah.

It was a routine trip to the drive-in, just like any other. I had thought about their double cheeseburger with extra onions all day at work. Once the clock struck five, I was on the road and heading towards my oasis in the middle of nowhere. I pulled into my usual spot and pressed the call button. I was expecting to hear the familiar tinny voice of one of my regular waitresses. But, instead, I heard the sweetest sound I'd ever heard coming through the small speaker.

'Hey sugar. What can I get ya?'

She practically cooed, not at all the business-like delivery most of the girls preferred. This girl took it to the next level and my pussy moistened in appreciation. I gave my order, reciting it from memory as I had eaten the same thing each time.

'Oooh. That sounds real good, sugar. I'll bring that right out to ya. Sit tight, baby.'

I could hardly believe my ears and, as I fished my wallet out of my pocket, I felt my cunt moisten just from the sound of her voice. I sat and watched the clock, hardly able to wait to see this new waitress in the flesh. I peered out the window for a long while, but eventually I gave up, my mind wandering to the Elvis music playing in the air. A flash brought my attention back, movement in the corner of my eye. My mouth fell open as I saw her, my breathing suddenly laboured and fast.

She was amazing. Her dark, seemingly jet-black hair was curled and coifed into the most perfect Bettie Page style I'd ever seen. Her hot pink uniform hugged each ample curve, her milky white breasts barely contained by the two top buttons. The skirt flared out at her hourglass hips, short enough to reveal the black garters that held up her pink and black striped tights. Instead of making a beeline for the car like all the other girls, she started spinning and twirling on her skates, which were shiny white patent leather with bright pink wheels. She held my tray in one hand, the other extended out at her side as she whirled my way, looking graceful and sexy as she approached. She did a full circle around my car before stopping at my window.

I drank her in as she stood there, her hip cocked; my food perched perfectly on the bright red tray. She leant down, bringing me face to face with her full cleavage that glimmered with glitter in the low light. I blatantly stared, unable to help myself. Her name patch said "Zarah", tackle-twilled in black thread. When my eyes finally moved up to her face, she was smiling; her blue eyes sparkling as she slowly chewed a cherry-scented piece of gum. I couldn't speak, but it didn't matter, she did all the talking.

'Hey sugar. Having a good night?'

I nodded, my words still failing me. As she gathered my order, I took a quick peek at her legs, the creamy white of her upper thigh a stark contrast to her stockings.

'So, I have a double cheeseburger, extra onions, double order of fries, and a chocolate malt shake. Did you need anything else, baby?'

Finally, my brain kicked in, and I managed to speak without sounding too stupid.

'Um, could I get a few extra napkins, please?'

'Oooh. Are you a messy girl?'

'I guess.'

Her smile kick-started my heart again and I smiled back as best I could. God, she was hot.

'Well, here you go, honey. If you need anything else, just press that little button and I'll come running, OK?'

'I will. Thanks, Zarah.'

'You're welcome, sugar.'

With that, she skated away, dropping down into a crouch before popping back up. That's when I saw it. Across the black bloomers that covered her fabulous full bottom, I saw the words "Sit On It" in glittery pink letters.

I could barely eat after that, but I managed somehow. I was hoping she would ask me my name but, coming out of her mouth, "sugar" sounded just fine.

Needless to say, after my first meeting with Zarah, I started showing up to the drive-in even more than usual. Can you blame a girl? Her look changed with the day, her pin-up style was flawless. I nearly choked when I saw her in pigtails, my hands itching to grab one in each hand. And, each and every time I showed up, there was a new message written on her ass. I lived for the moment when it was revealed, the anticipation of what it might say making my mouth water almost more than the damn burgers.

It didn't take her long to notice my increased attendance, but I was beyond caring if it made me look desperate or foolish. I flirted shamelessly with Zarah every chance I got, and asked for her each time another girl answered the call button. Eventually, she caught on to my little game and one late night, very close to closing time, she upped the ante.

'Well, well, if it isn't my favourite regular customer. Are you stalking me, sugar? Am I going to have to start calling the cops?'

I laughed and, thankfully, she did too. The pigtails were back and I had never been gladder. She twirled her finger in the dark strands, making it hard for me to concentrate on being witty.

'Don't do that. I swear I'm just here for the burgers.'

'Honey, if that were true, you could get them from Daisy or Mona or Karen. Why always me?'

Her legs were covered with classic seamed stockings. How was a girl supposed to function with that going on? The rest of the drive-in was deserted. It was just her and me, everyone else having gone home for the night.

'What can I say, Zarah? You put on a better show than the others.'

'Well, thanks, sugar. But, trust me, you ain't seen nothing yet.'

'What do you mean?'

'Let me get you another milkshake and I'll show you.'

She skated away and I finally took a breath. She disappeared into the drive-in and the next thing I knew, it was dark, all the lights having gone off at once. Then, dim blue and white light filled the little area where my car sat and *Peggy Sue* started playing through the speakers. I watched the door to the drive-in, but she shocked me by skating past the car the other way. I craned my neck trying to see her, and when I finally caught a glimpse, she was beckoning me with a crooked finger.

I got out of the car, leaning against the back of my station wagon, my eyes never leaving her. Instead of her usual uniform, she was only wearing a black lace bra that did wonderful things to her already ample chest. A navel ring punctuated the gentle curve of her stomach and barely covering her sexy wide hips was a tiny plaid skirt that immediately sent my mind back to my Catholic school days. Her legs were covered with black and white knee socks, her skates now adorned with black wheels.

She started skating closer to me, but as soon as she got near enough to touch, she quickly moved away. My pussy was aching as she twirled and spun to the music, swaying her hips and shaking her tits in my direction. I was getting anxious, but Zarah was clearly in charge. She pivoted on her skates, so her back was to me. Slowly, so damn slowly, she started to bend over, her hands sliding down her legs. That's when I saw it. The words written across her ass were the words I'd wanted to read since the first time I saw her. In blue satin writing, it read simply, "Fuck Me Sugar".

I could stay put no longer and I pushed off my car, getting to Zarah in about four steps, her back still to me. Wrapping my arms around her waist, she tipped her head back against my shoulder. Her breathy voice filled my ears, taking me back to that first time I'd heard her sweetly through the speaker.

'I think I've made you wait long enough, sugar. By the way, I made these panties just for you.'

I ran my hands up her soft skin, until they were cupping her huge tits, still contained by the silky lace cups. She grinded her ass against me, making my knees buckle a bit as I teased her hard nipples through the soft fabric. Zarah spun around, her arms reaching behind her back. Her bra slid away and I finally saw her big, beautiful tits. Her nipples peaked in the cool night air, and I gasped when she ran her thumbs over her own nipples, licking her red lips just right. But she wasn't done. Her hands ran down her body until she reached under her skirt and started to pull down her special panties. Stepping gracefully out of them, even in skates, she stood back up, tossing them to me with a giggle. I instinctively caught them, rubbing the silky, soft fabric between my fingers.

'So, what are we waiting for, honey? I think the panties are pretty clear.'

I turned away from her just long enough to pull open the tailgate to my station wagon. I heard her wheels clicking on the blacktop and she moved right past me into the car, easing back on the blanket that was always in the back of the station wagon. Her abundant thighs parted, revealing her bare pussy, clearly wet. Her fingers eased her lips apart and started toying with her swollen clit, while I stood there dumbfounded. God, she was really fucking hot.

'Come on, sugar. Don't be shy now.'

I crawled in after her and she guided me right in between her legs. My lips and tongue went immediately to work, tasting her salty flavour and enjoying the squirming action of her hips. Every time her legs moved, her skates banged around, making loud sounds against the inside of my car. It should have been distracting, but it only served as a reminder of her sexy moves and made me even hotter. I dipped two fingers inside Zarah, her throaty moans filling my car with each stuttering thrust. Her pussy was so very warm and wet; clutching and pulling each time I twisted my wrist. My tongue and thumb alternated moving over her clit and soon her hands were twined in my hair, pulling and moving me exactly how she wanted me. My own pussy was throbbing but I kept all my attention on her.

Zarah's voice cracked as she spoke between moans, clearly enjoying herself.

'I want more, sugar. Fill me up so I can come all over that pretty face of yours.'

I added a third finger to her sweet pussy and she gasped. My eyes were transfixed, staring at her wet hole opening up to take me inside. My thumb returned to her clit, rubbing small circles as she rocked her hips back and forth. She bucked against me, her cries turning from sweet to guttural as I plunged my fingers as deep as I could.

'More, baby. More.'

Her hips started pushing up faster as I slipped a fourth finger inside her. Zarah yelled out, her voice echoing all around the car. She started playing with her own nipples and moving around in a crazy figure eight. As much as I was enjoying the show, I couldn't resist another taste of her. My tongue slid over her clit, my fingers pumping in and out of her moist cunt at a faster and faster pace.

'Come on sugar, fuck me like you mean it. Like you've been dying to since you first saw me.'

I did as she asked and finger-fucked her pussy as hard and fast as I could manage. I sucked on her clit, flicking the hard bud with my tongue as I thrust my fingers nice and deep.

'Oh yeah, baby. That's perfect. Oh God, yeah, baby. Yes. Yes, yes, yesyesyesyesyes.'

She was almost chanting as she came, her sweet pussy squeezing around my hand, her whole body trembling as I fucked her through her screaming orgasm, her cunt soaking my fingers with her juice. I pulled back and saw the gorgeous look on her face as her body slowly loosening its hold on me, her hips slowly coming to a stop. She pulled me up her body and kissed me hard, my face still stained with her essence. Her breathing started to slow and she planted small kisses all over my cheek.

'Damn, sugar. That was amazing.'

'Thanks.'

'Don't move, baby. I'll be right back.'

'Where are you going, Zarah?'

Zahra didn't answer me and she didn't bother getting dressed before she skated away and into the diner. She returned quickly, two cups in her hands, and I smiled as she spun around three times before coming to a stop and climbing back in the car. She handed me one of the cups, and then took a sexy sip of her own, licking her lips as she finished.

'I almost forgot your milkshake, baby.'

'Thanks.'

I took a long drink of chocolate goodness and looked up at her. She leant in for a kiss, then gave me a wink.

'Drink up, sugar. You need your strength. Because you and I are just getting started.'

I pulled her into an embrace, kissing her and tasting sweet strawberries.

'I can't wait, baby.'

Damsel
by Jade Taylor

The thunder cracked loudly overhead as I walked outside, and I smiled at last.

Finally it would rain.

The heat had been oppressive for weeks, and I woke every morning as tired as I'd been the night before, exhausted from another night of tossing and turning relentlessly.

The days were spent trying to keep cool, both literally and figuratively, as the office filled with cheap electrical fans, bad tempers, and sharp words.

So when the boss asked me to stay late I only begrudgingly agreed, wishing instead I could get home for a long, cool shower and a long, cold drink.

I almost made it to my car before the heavens opened.

I stood still for a moment and let the rain soak me, glad to be feeling cooler. Then I dashed for the car and laughed like a child as I splashed through the puddles that had quickly appeared.

I started the engine and turned on the air conditioning; despite the torrential downpour my clothes were almost dry already, it was so hot.

The rain was thick and fast as I drove off slowly, my wipers swishing back and forth in a furious fashion.

What a crap end to a crap day.

All I wanted to do was get home and forget about it all. Then I saw her.

She was standing by the bus stop, thoroughly drenched in a gorgeous summer dress that provided her little protection against the rain.

Thoughts of dashing home left my mind immediately, as other, more base thoughts replaced them.

I'd always wanted to rescue a damsel in distress.

Call it old-fashioned, call it some sort of domineering streak, blame it on watching too many romantic comedies where coming to the aid of a girl in some kind of trouble led to the hottest sex scene ever, but the scenario had always appealed.

So when I saw her on the other side of the road, obviously in need of help, I wasn't sure whether she was real, or a fantasy.

She was absolutely soaked through, looking pretty miserable, the floaty little dress she'd no doubt picked out when the sun was shining seeming suddenly like a poor choice. The shortness of it showed off her sexy legs, though, and the way it was sticking to her displayed her amazing figure, with pert breasts and an amazing arse.

Her petite stature and the floral dress lent her an air of girlish innocence, but the body underneath was more than womanly.

Her cute elfin cut meant at least her brunette curls weren't getting plastered to her face, and as she lifted her face as if to beg the rain to please stop I saw her big, wide, chocolate-coloured eyes.

She might have been feeling cold, wet, and fed up – but she looked fucking hot.

Here was a damsel I really wanted to rescue.

Quickly, I glanced into my rear-view mirror and did a three-point turn, then drove back down the road and pulled up next to the bus stop.

She was even more attractive close up, and despite how bad my day had been I suddenly felt a surge of lust, a blast of adrenaline, a heat flooding through my body that had nothing to do with the weather.

She could make everything better.

I smiled as I opened the window.

'Hi, I was just wondering if I could give you a lift somewhere?'

She hesitated, thinking perhaps it was a strange offer. But I was a woman; I didn't look like a serial killer, just someone trying to be friendly.

She wouldn't know I had ulterior motives.

'It's OK, I'm sure the bus will be here soon,' she said, but she didn't sound convinced, more like she'd declined because she thought it was the polite thing to do.

'It's no bother,' I added, aware that she was uncertain. 'Which way are you going?'

'Just near the town centre?'

That was where I had just come from.

'That's where I'm going,' I lied. 'Why don't you jump in?'

She hesitated and looked up the street as if expecting the bus to magically appear. Then she ran her hands through her hair, and then climbed into the car.

As she sat next to me I noticed I could see nipples, hard and erect, through the flimsy material of her dress.

I wanted to see them without the dress.

I felt myself getting wet.

'Are you OK?' she asked, and I thought that maybe she'd caught me looking.

I blushed. 'Yep.' I paused a moment, then said, 'I like your dress.'

She smiled, 'Thanks, though I'm beginning to regret

73

wearing it today.'

I said nothing, thinking that maybe I wouldn't have spotted her if she'd been wearing something more suitable for the weather; even in a light raincoat she would have been unlikely to catch my eye.

I drove back to the town centre silently as she chatted to me. I tried to respond, but I couldn't. Lust had me tongue-tied; I didn't want to make small talk about the weather, I just wanted to touch her.

For some reason her being in the car with me made me strangely nervous too, and I wondered if she was babbling for the same reason.

It felt like there was some tension between us, like the feeling you get before a storm, like there's static in the air, and I wondered if she felt it too, or if it was just my wishful thinking.

We arrived at her flat quicker than I'd hoped.

I parked the car slowly, unwilling to let this encounter end.

I turned off the engine, and was relieved when she didn't jump straight out.

'Would you like a coffee?' she said, turning to me. 'To say thank you for the lift?'

'I'd love that,' I said, even as my mind raced to the many other ways I'd prefer her to thank me, to the way being invited in for coffee could be so often interpreted.

I followed her up the stairs to her flat, watching her peachy arse, fighting the urge to touch it with every step she took.

I had no idea if she was interested, if she was straight, gay or bi, but as I followed into her flat I decided I couldn't let this opportunity pass me by.

I felt wet and horny at the thought of my fantasy coming true, of finally fucking my damsel in distress.

I had to make a move.

She went into the kitchen to put the kettle on, then came back to ask me, 'How do you like it?'

She smiled in a way that made me think she was flirting.

I took a chance, and stepped closer.

She didn't move away.

I reached for the top button of her dress.

'You really ought to get out of these wet clothes.'

She said nothing, and I opened it. I hesitated, half sure would stop me, but instead she smiled, so I opened the next button, then the next, until she stood there with her dress unbuttoned to waist level.

Her bra was pink and flimsy, and the rainwater had made it transparent, clearly showing me her beautiful breasts and her erect nipples.

Now I wasn't sure whether it was the cold or the excitement that had them hard.

I cupped her breasts, running my thumb over her nipples as she sighed loudly.

I felt my pulse beating between my legs as the blood rushed to my clit.

She was so gorgeous.

I moved closer to kiss her, feeling her damp skin touching mine, as my mouth finally met hers.

This wasn't a shy, tentative kiss; instead it seemed we were both inflamed with passion as we somehow tumbled back, her onto the sofa and me kneeling before her.

I pulled away from kissing her to push up her skirt, smiling at the sight of her in such disarray, her face a picture of lust and her skirt bunched around her waist.

I wanted her so badly.

Slowly, I trailed my hands up her legs and up to her hips, then roughly tugged her panties down.

Still she said nothing, lifting her arse to allow me to pull them off more easily.

The silence and her passivity only served to make me more aroused.

It was as if she truly was a damsel in distress who would allow her hero to do anything to her.

With that in mind I pulled her legs forward, so she sank deeper back into the sofa.

I stopped to take in this picture of dishevelment, with her legs splayed and her most intimate places fully exposed to me.

I'd never felt more turned on.

I bent my head down, slowly kissing up the inside of her thigh. She moaned, almost impatiently, and I laughed as I continued teasing her.

As she sighed again I put a hand between my thighs, slowly starting to rub my own clit.

With my other hand I teased her, watching her cunt as much as I watched her face for her reaction, watching as her cunt grew wet and her face grew flushed.

I was just as wet as I snaked a hand inside my panties, rubbing at my clit more quickly now as I leant forward to lick her.

She gasped loudly, though I'd hardly touched her.

'Please,' she sighed, and I increased the pressure on her clit, my tongue swirling circles on and around it as her hips moved to lift her up, to press against me harder.

My hand moved quicker and I came under my own expert touch, refusing to let my shuddering body distract me from lapping at her until she felt the same.

'Fuck,' she gasped loudly, breathless and frantic, as she came, juddering beneath my touch.

For a moment we were still, and then she stood, taking my hand.

'My turn,' she said, leading me to the bedroom.

She stripped me off quickly and roughly, suddenly in charge, and I smiled at how her seeming shyness had been just pretence.

The innocent damsel from the bus stop was replaced now by a vixen who knew exactly what she wanted.

My clit twitched at the thought.

She moved me to lie back on the bed and then reached for a vibrator from her drawer.

'Is this OK?' she asked, and I nodded dumbly.

It was only a tiny thing, but when she turned it on I realised how powerful it was as she trailed it across my breasts, across my nipples, down my stomach, and then placed it directly on my clit.

'I want to watch you come,' she said, and though I'd always been the dominant one in my fantasies I was happy to play along with whatever she wanted.

I liked how the roles had changed.

Now she watched my face and my cunt as I felt the powerful vibrations against me, as she trailed a hand almost nonchalantly across my body, teasing my nipples with a gentle touch and then tweaking them roughly.

The combination of the pain and the pleasure only intensified the sensations in my clit.

'Please,' I pleaded now; as she bent down to kiss me, she pressed the vibrator against my clit harder, and I gasped out my orgasm as our mouths met once more.

I waited in silence as she then sat at the end of the bed, watching her as she watched me, her legs wide open so I could see everything, and put the vibe against her clit until she came again.

She was not the delicate flower I'd expected.

I liked that.

'I thought you were shy.' I grinned, crawling down the

bed to rest my head on her thigh. 'I wasn't sure if you were even interested.'

'You thought this was some straight girl fantasy?' she asked teasingly.

'I thought you were a damsel in distress,' I admitted, blushing.

'No, I'm more the wolf in sheep's clothing.' She laughed. 'And I don't have straight girl fantasies; mine are a different type entirely.' Her hand ran up my thigh.

'I'd realised.'

'Now I really ought to get out of these wet clothes,' she said as she unbuttoned her dress completely, then walked to the bathroom and turned on the shower.

I lay back on the bed, smiling.

'Are you coming?' she shouted through to me in a voice laden with innuendo.

'I hope so.' I laughed, and followed her quickly.

Peaches
by Beverly Langland

Tanya was waiting for Georgina at the door, her eyes as bright as a puppy's, her expression just as eager. Normally she would have helped Georgina with her coat, but being a Friday she simply stood to the side and waited patiently to gain the older woman's attention. She was dressed much as Georgina had left her – hands bound behind her back, ankles shackled together with a length of pristine (and rather heavy) chain. It had been Georgina's pleasure to bind Tanya before leaving for the office that morning, and she fully intended to keep her live-in lover bound and shackled for the remainder of the weekend. A treat for both.

Georgina's darling girl was always pleased to welcome her home, but she could tell that today Tanya was especially excited. The girl's nipples were hard for one – Georgina could clearly see the fixed points standing proud on Tanya's pert breasts through the thin fabric of her dress – and she was fidgeting impatiently, no doubt keen for Georgina to remove her chastity belt.

Georgina sighed. One of the benefits of having such a young lover was the girl's boundless enthusiasm for all things in general and, in Tanya's case, her pursuit of sexual fulfilment. Keeping a young lover maintained the pretence of youthfulness for Georgina, but sometimes (just sometimes) she looked into the girl's bright, brown eyes, stroked Tanya's perfect, pale complexion, and all that stirred were feelings of regret. Not that Georgina would ever complain about passionate sex. She'd endured her fill of disinterested partners over the years. Contrary to what she read in the tabloids, not all lesbians were sex-starved vixens. Georgina smiled. She may have come close when she was much younger, but then, she had been trying to make a statement – had been striking back at her parents in the only way she knew how. Her parents had thrown her out of their suburban house (her home) and disowned the confused teenager, as was the way of the world in those days. Her rebellion achieved nothing, of course, except damaging her respectful reputation – and reputations counted for everything back then.

Georgina thought she understood how Tanya must feel. Sex was a form of expression for the girl, perhaps considering their particular arrangement, the only way. Over the years, the older woman had grown comfortable with her lifestyle. Two women living together was now quite acceptable if, sadly, not the norm. Though Tanya wasn't a traditional housewife. Not Georgina's wife at all. She was not even her partner. Until recently, Georgina had considered the girl more of a houseguest, a transient in her rather complicated life. Yet, Tanya had been living under her roof for over a year and the beautiful blonde angel didn't look like she intended to move on any time soon. Not that Georgina made it easy for Tanya to move anywhere.

She untied the girl's gag. Tanya stretched her mouth, and let out one of her cute little puppy dog sighs – spoiled only by the snap of a terrier. 'You're late again!'

'Nice to see you too. No kiss for Mummy?'

'Yes, of course. Sorry, it's just that I've missed you.'

'And I've missed you too, sweetie. Difficult day?'

Tanya turned, showing Georgina the chafe marks caused by pulling against the rough ropes. The girl's arms were blotchy red from where she had been struggling to free herself. 'Oh dear. I see you've been enjoying yourself while I've been busy working.' Tanya blushed. Bondage had only recently become a permanent part of their lives. Sex was often an integral element, but bondage actually transcended sex for the two women. Taming Tanya had almost become a way of life, although Georgina's first experiments with bondage had started 20 years previously with little Susie.

Her name was actually Susan, and she was a woman only a few years younger than Georgina, but she willingly slipped into the role of young Susie when they played their bondage games together. Susan was a masochistic submissive looking for a permanent partner – a mistress as well as a lover. Georgina had been merely curious. Nevertheless, Susan taught Georgina how to control another human being, taught her the power of sexual *persuasion*. The two women had fun while the novelty lasted, but ultimately Susan left Georgina to continue her search elsewhere. Georgina was not strict enough for Susan's tastes. While she had found administering certain "inducements" and punishments exciting, especially for one new to the concept, she could not force herself to hurt Susan. Despite her lover's constant urging. Georgina was not a sadist – at least, she had not believed so at the time. She was not even a proper domme. Yet, Georgina had learnt the power and enjoyment of control.

Susan's departure had truly saddened Georgina, but the notion that there must be women into bondage without a deep need for pain had buoyed her spirits. Not that bondage was pain free – something to which anyone who has been tied for any length of time would no doubt testify. Luckily, Tanya was one of those young women who liked to feel owned. Wrapping her tight and keeping her safe were the same. She was a runaway teenager whom Georgina had found sleeping rough. The older woman had taken pity on Tanya and bought her home. Initially, she had regarded the girl as more of a pet than a lover. And now ... Well, Tanya was a blessing to have around the house. Compared with Georgina, she was a domestic goddess, and her feelings for Georgina seemed genuine. At least, the girl knew she was on to a good thing. Whatever Tanya did (good or bad) she designed for Georgina's pleasure.

However, the young woman did have a wicked streak. She might look like an angel but, like all pets, she could be naughty and mischievous to the point of testing Georgina's limited patience. At such times, Georgina would give Tanya a thorough spanking, having quickly discovered that the girl responded well to that particular humiliation, almost as if she needed to prove how much she would endure for the sake of her lover. Just as well, for Georgina expected nothing less than Tanya's utter devotion.

As always, the dinner table was set and there were some delicious aromas coming from the kitchen. Tanya had become amazingly adept at cooking with her limited mobility. Little concession had been made in the kitchen to make managing easier, and yet Tanya managed to surprise Georgina time and time again. Georgina made herself comfortable while Tanya brought in the dish – a beef casserole of some kind. The girl sat waiting patiently for Georgina to start. Georgina fed Tanya her dinner as she ate her own. Most of the time she used a fork, but occasionally the older woman used her fingers to put morsels into the girl's mouth. Each bite Tanya accepted as a gift, delight in her eyes. She licked Georgina's fingers clean, often running her tongue between the digits, sometimes sucking one or two fingers into her petite mouth. Each mouthful seemed to drive the girl deeper into her fantasy until Georgina had finished.

'That was delicious. Any dessert?'

Tanya's eyes lit up. 'Yes. I have a surprise for you!' The girl looked towards the kitchen. 'May I?'

Georgina nodded her assent, and Tanya almost skipped off in delight. Georgina was reaching for her mail, laid out neatly on the side table, when Tanya put the blindfold over her eyes. 'What's this?' It took a few moments for Georgina to register that the little vixen had somehow untied her arms. So that's why her skin was so chafed.

'As I said, a surprise.' Tanya took Georgina's hand and led her into the kitchen. After a few minutes, she pressed a spoon to Georgina's lips. The woman opened her mouth and the girl fed her some rum-flavoured fruit. 'I've made a fruit cocktail.'

'That's dessert?' Georgina was a little disappointed, especially after the wonderful Beef Stroganoff she had enjoyed, and Tanya's promise of a surprise. The young woman was usually much more creative in the kitchen.

'Be patient! I just need to warm the oven.' At which point Tanya slipped her hand between Georgina's legs to cup the woman's sex, and vigorously started rubbing.

'This is your idea of dessert?'

'I haven't finished.'

Georgina waited patiently, allowing Tanya to fondle her, indulging the girl for a few minutes more – besides, Tanya's touch was always enjoyable and was growing more so by the second. The girl's small hands had always excited Georgina. There were times when (if in the right mood) she would encourage the girl to squeeze the whole of her hand into her wet cunt. The idea had come from a lesbian porn film Georgina had watched, and had been one of her unfulfilled fantasies. She had been surprised the first time Tanya managed the deed, the shock of the hand completely filling her sending Georgina spiralling into orgasm. The mixture of pain and pleasure was something she had grown to enjoy since – a special treat. The thought of having Tanya's hand inside her sex made Georgina shiver, so she didn't object when Tanya undid the zip of her trousers, unbuttoned them … Sure enough, the girl slipped her hand inside her panties, curling her wonderful fingers into Georgina's soft flesh. Georgina was already hot and wet and Tanya took full advantage of the lubrication. Georgina closed her eyes, when the girl's hand deserted her to return moments later with something nestled in her palm – something soft and squishy.

'What's that?'

'Peaches.' Tanya pressed the fruit against Georgina's sex, mashing the peaches against her already moist lips.

'Don't! I'm not sure I like it.'

'Then you'll hate this!'

Georgina gasped as what felt like an entire can of peaches filled her panties. Juice ran down her legs in cold rivulets, enough to fill her shoes. 'Tanya! You'll ruin my suit.'

For once, Tanya ignored her protests, kneading the soft fruit halves into the older woman's sex, deliberately pushing large pieces between her tingling lips. Tanya pressed down on Georgina's shoulders. 'Lie down.'

Georgina obeyed, forcing the protests from her mind. She lay on the kitchen floor, somewhat shell-shocked by Tanya's sudden onslaught. The girl had never rebelled like this before, but Georgina rather liked the notion. She lifted her bottom as Tanya pulled off her expensive trousers and panties, silently praying they weren't ruined. She had a mind to remove the blindfold, a little surprised that she hadn't already. Only removing it would spoil Tanya's surprise, and despite her misgivings, Georgina was aroused. A vision of Tanya munching away at those embedded peaches got her pulse racing.

Without warning, a sudden deluge engulfed her, soaking her from midriff upwards. 'Surprise!' A second downpour followed the first, almost taking the breath out of Georgina. The sticky liquid was full of lumps. *Fruit cocktail*! The concoction covered her – fruit was in her hair, juice soaking through her clothes.

'Have you gone completely mad?'

'Mad for you. This is what happens when you leave me stewing for days on end. You're meant to play with your toys now and again!' Tanya's weight settled over Georgina's body. The girl sat astride her, lewdly rubbing her encased pussy against Georgina's sex, mashing her pubic bone hard against her throbbing clitoris. 'Now, I'm going to eat this fruit and then I'm going to eat your cunt. Any objections?'

'No.' Georgina's voice sounded broken.

Tanya lay forward and started to slide over Georgina's wet body. Georgina was in two minds – whether to lie still or to wrap her arms around her lover and encourage her gyrations. She was enjoying playing the passive partner for once, aroused by Tanya's inventiveness and apparent disregard for her clothes – for Georgina's authority. The boundaries of their relationship had shifted, if only temporarily, and the danger if Georgina moved was that Tanya might fall back into her submissive role. Georgina groaned as the girl slid down her body. She had been enjoying the weight on top of her, loving the press of

85

Tanya's breasts against her own.

True to her word, Tanya began to eat the fruit. She started at Georgina's feet, removing the woman's shoes, licking the juice from between her toes, and running her tongue over her sensitive sole. Tanya's tongue slowly worked its way up Georgina's body. Every time she came to a piece of fruit, she sucked it into her mouth, sighing with obvious pleasure. Tanya spent considerable time on Georgina's inner thighs, knowing from experience that the touch of her tongue on that part of the woman's body drove her crazy with desire.

The girl inched ever closer to Georgina's pussy. Only she deliberately bypassed her sex, much to Georgina's chagrin, pausing at her belly button to drink the pool gathered there. Tanya started to unbutton Georgina's blouse, but after the first, she ripped the folds apart, sending the buttons flying. Tanya pushed Georgina's bra upwards, exposing her breasts. Georgina's nipples were hard, growing harder as Tanya went straight for them with mouth and teeth. Georgina groaned. Of all her erogenous zones, her nipples were perhaps her most sensitive. Perhaps that's why Tanya paid particular attention to them, spending much more time than she needed to remove the fruit and juices. The shock waves sent to Georgina's clitoris made the little nubbin so hard that it hurt.

In fact, the call of her clitoris had grown so great Georgina had to fight the urge to touch. She wanted to so badly. The anticipation had been building ever since Tanya first started her journey; now her need reached unprecedented levels – but how much better it would feel when Tanya arrived at her final destination, as she surely must. The girl seemed to know Georgina's every sensitive spot. She explored them all at her leisure.

'I love eating you!'

Tanya was clearly enjoying being in control. The trouble for Georgina was Tanya wasn't eating her pussy, and her need was growing increasingly desperate. She was in danger of losing her patience. Of course, Georgina could flip the girl over and end the agony of waiting. She could easily pin down that lithe body and sit on Tanya's face, and then she would teach the little bitch how to eat pussy. Perhaps she would piss in the girl's mouth and remind Tanya who was actually in control here! Yet, the frenzied thought passed, leaving Georgina shocked that she had even considered such a taboo thing.

Perhaps she *had* been neglectful of late. Perhaps she deserved to be punished in some small way, for despite Tanya's insistence that the ambush was a surprise, the girl's dynamism almost felt like a punishment. Her errant tongue was such sweet torture – like when Susie used to bind Georgina tight and tease her mercilessly for hours. Georgina had thought those days had passed. Control was her *modus operandi* now, obedience her byword, but she had been thinking more and more about Susie recently, imagining the filthy things they used to do together. Georgina shook her head. She didn't want such thoughts to enter her clean, controlled, safe little life. Yet, now this …

Tanya stuffed a handful of peaches inside the older woman, inserting them with her slick fingers while her thumb sought out Georgina's beating clitoris. Georgina's reaction was instantaneous. She threw her hips up off the floor trying to drive Tanya's fingers in deeper. She was coming, and coming hard, thrashing around on the kitchen floor as Tanya's fingers pummelled deep into her cunt. Her orgasm seemed to go on for ever, the intensity of her climax torture in itself. Yet, Georgina's sweet agony didn't stop there. The girl still worked her thumb on her clitoris, driving the older woman crazy. Georgina had barely recovered her breath when the familiar clenching inside her vagina started again, the feeling growing ever more intense until Georgina was throwing her head from side to side wildly.

As she approached another orgasm, Tanya suddenly removed her fingers – perhaps a deliberate attempt to turn the tables on the older woman and tease Georgina for a change. Georgina didn't seem to welcome the hiatus. She started pleading with Tanya to take her over the edge. The blonde angel merely gave a wicked smile, enjoying her lover's sweet agony.

'I've been waiting all day to eat you.'

'Well, fucking get on with it!'

'All in good time, my love. All in good time.'

Tanya moved back to Georgina's knee, eventually licking her way up the insides of Georgina's thighs. The lack of a second orgasm had driven Georgina to heights of passion she hadn't achieved for a long time. Higher and higher the girl pushed her, so that when Tanya finally placed her lips against her drenched pussy, the woman exploded once again in a fit of ecstasy, bucking her hips frantically against Tanya's pretty face.

Undeterred, Tanya continued her assault, running her tongue from Georgina's clitoris all the way to her arse and everything in between. Georgina came and came again. It had been an eternity since she had experienced multiple orgasms of this magnitude. Her pleasure went on for so long; it felt like Tanya had her face in her vagina for hours. Eventually, the girl pulled her face away from the throbbing mess between Georgina's thighs and crawled up her trembling body. Tanya's face was glistening, her mouth coated with a heady mixture of peach juice and

Georgina's copious secretions. A fragment of peach lay on Tanya's lip, and when the girl smiled Georgina noticed strands of fruit had caught between her teeth.

The couple kissed, and Georgina tasted what Tanya had tasted moments before – a cocktail made in heaven. Although, following the afterglow of their lovemaking, the cold reality of sticky fruit cocktail seeped into her consciousness. Tanya grew agitated also. To Georgina's knowledge, the girl had not climaxed and she would be eager for her own fulfilment. Tanya stood and helped Georgina to her feet. Face to face, they kissed again.

'Carry me to bed,' Tanya whispered.

'Carry you?'

Tanya nodded and all but jumped into Georgina's arms as the older woman swept her hand beneath the girl's legs. She had one arm draped over Georgina's shoulders, looking up at her lover with those puppy brown eyes. *Fuck me*, they implored. Surprised by the girl's lightness, Georgina marched into the bedroom, naked from the waist down, leaving behind a trail of broken peaches in the hall. She laid Tanya on the bed and quickly removed the girl's chastity belt. Tanya waited patiently as always, watching as Georgina undressed, fully revealing her breasts, the nipples still hard and erect.

Georgina climbed onto the bed at Tanya's feet, taking hold of the girl's ankles to spread her legs wide and she inched between them. Tanya looked up at Georgina, her surprise showing. She mimicked holding up a camera. 'Quick! Take a picture. I want to remember this moment. I can't believe you're actually going to go down on me.'

'Why shouldn't I?'

'Well, for a lesbian, you don't do cunnilingus all that often.'

Tanya lifted the hem of her dress well above her waist,

raised both her knees, allowing Georgina total access to her tender, glistening pussy. It looked scrumptious – groomed and well-tended especially for her lover. Not for the first time, Georgina thanked the heavens for her luck. Tanya gazed at the dark-haired woman from between her knees, Georgina maintaining eye contact as she edged forward. 'I could lick you from now until the end of eternity,' she said, taking hold of Tanya's knees and pushing them apart. She leant forward and kissed the girl's inner thigh, moving her face closer to begin lashing away at Tanya's soft, velvety slit with her tongue.

The girl moaned and arched her back in response, craning her neck, trying to watch. 'I love you,' she said.

Georgina withdrew her mouth from the girl's succulent folds only long enough to reply. 'I love you too, peaches.' She licked again.

'Peaches?'

Georgina lifted her head again and smiled. 'Seems appropriate, and you *are* as sweet as a peach.'

An instant later, she was dining on Tanya's delicious pussy yet again. Georgina worked over Tanya's clitoris, swiping the sensitive nub of skin with her tongue in a hot, frenzied attack. Wanting to increase the girl's pleasure, the experienced woman changed tack – first tonguing deep into Tanya's pussy, then dabbing at her clitoris, keeping her guessing. Tanya was already moaning her approval.

Georgina loved watching the girl's beautiful body squirm and writhe upon the bed. When she inserted a pair of fingers between the moist folds of her pussy, Tanya's excitement level seemed to triple. Now under an erotic onslaught from Georgina's tongue as well as two fingers, she grasped her lover's hair, pulling Georgina's head closer and the girl let out a loud, shrill moan.

'Oh Georgie!' Tanya was coming hard. 'Georgina!'

Showered and clean and nestled between fresh sheets, the two women snuggled, Georgina reflecting on Tanya's unusual behaviour. The older woman was truly in love and the thought of possibly losing Tanya filled her heart with dread. What did all the dreams and daydreams of Susie mean? Was she regressing as she grew older, or did she simply resent her lover's youthfulness? Sometimes she just wanted to slap Tanya's beautiful face, to punish the girl for reminding Georgina of her own failings. The repulsive notion made her heart falter. She swallowed hard.

Tanya, pressed tight against Georgina's breast, looked up as if sensing the missed heartbeat, her puppy-dog expression already back in place.

'Bind me,' she whispered. 'I want to feel the bite of your ropes.'

Georgina didn't argue. There were plenty of ropes in the bedside table. She bound her lover tight, passing the last rope between Tanya's luscious thighs, making certain the rough hessian split the girl's sex to chafe against her clitoris. Georgina gave the rope a testing tug, causing Tanya to moan and edge closer. She wrapped the end of the rope in her hand, gripping tight. Perhaps tomorrow she would punish the girl for her insolence. When was the last time she had spanked her?

Georgina's mind strayed to all the nasty things she would do to Tanya. Didn't she still have nipple clamps somewhere? And there were other items in Susan's box in the garage. She was not as shocked as she thought she should be. She knew she now had it in her to hurt the girl. Perhaps Susie had known all those years ago. Perhaps. Yet, she had to tread carefully. Tanya might be her last chance for lasting love.

Georgina stayed awake until she heard the soft shallowness of Tanya's breathing and knew the girl was asleep. She pulled the rope tight. There was no way she was going to let go of her, whatever happened.

Seven More Minutes in Heaven
by M. Marie

Seeing her again for the first time after our separation, I was amazed at the changes six years apart had made.

In fact, I didn't even recognise her at first. Scanning the thick crowd of friends and strangers at Leanne's Victoria Day party, my eyes had dismissively slid right over her before something about the tilt of her chin and the curve of her lips had given my heartstrings a nostalgic tug. Turning my attention back to the plump, solitary woman standing alone on the far side of the room, my breath caught in my throat as recognition struck me.

It was Carla.

The changes in her were startling. As long as I had known Carla Ramones, she had embodied the word *provocative*. With sharp angles and long, endless legs, she could walk into any room and draw all eyes to her. Now, though, she was a wallflower clinging to the perimeter of the room while the party played out around her. I moved closer, both disturbed and drawn to the perversions of her old personality that this new Carla embraced.

She still wore her hair short, but now the rebellious, galvanic Mohawk she had been known for throughout college was grown out into a generic, boring bob. Her hair was still dyed, as well, but whereas she used to opt for vivid reds and vibrant blondes when she was younger,

Carla was now hiding her face behind a thick fringe of lifeless brown hair. Looking at her from across the room, I refused to entertain the thought that this might be my wild Carla's *natural* hair colour.

Our mutual friends had diligently kept me up to date on Carla's life since our break-up a few weeks after graduating from college. I knew she'd settled down with a man she met through work; I had heard about her marriage and its collapse two years later. Along with the ex-husband, I'd been told she had children now, and all the financial and emotional burdens those types of commitments carried. I could see the truth in the rumours. Her eyes were tired and her appearance was worn.

Still, she was wearing a wedding ring on her left hand. The stubbornness of that continued display made my chest ache for the hopeful girl I had loved years before; I set down my drink, and made my way across the room.

The music was loud and the room pulsed with energy and expectation. As I threaded my way through the dancers, while Leanne's playlist blasted out an unfamiliar remix, I noticed Carla's eyes land on me and widen in surprise. I felt a wide grin slide across my face; I was happy she still recognised me after all these years. I too had transformed myself since we had parted.

Carla made no attempt to hide her roving eyes as I approached. Her gaze slid slowly down my body, then back up to meet my gaze as I stopped a few steps away.

'Marie.' Her tone was reserved, but the slight tremble in her lower lip gave away her nervousness. I felt a hint of the same anxiety tightening my throat, but swallowed it down in order to greet her in return. I don't quite recall what small talk I made, but I still vividly remember her abrupt laughter and the way the tired wrinkles around her mouth suddenly smoothed out into the laugh lines I remembered so well.

And in that moment, I wanted her more than I ever had before.

Using the excuse of the loud music, I stepped closer and pressed my lips to her left ear to whisper, 'Let's find a quiet spot to catch up.'

Whether she suspected my true intentions or not, Carla nodded towards a nondescript door near the staircase. *Perfect.* Taking the lead, I reached down for her hand and guided her through the other guests. When we reached our destination, I cast a quick look around before pulling her into the closet with, no doubt, a ridiculously unrestrained grin on my face.

As soon as we were both squeezed inside, I pulled the door shut behind us. The darkness settled around us expectantly and her warm hand in my grasp made my breath hitch. It all felt so familiar. My thoughts flashed to a similar situation in our second year of college, when we had both been so young and still so eager to explore and experiment with both ourselves and each other. With a feeling of nostalgia, I recalled the splash of light under the closet door as we awkwardly pressed together. I remembered my nervous fumbling and Carla's confident instructions, the echoes of faint pop music and the stimulating sound of our loud, heavy breathing. And, above all, I called to mind the giggles of girls' voices from the other side of the door as our friends and sorority sisters gleefully counted down the final few seconds of our first seven minutes in "heaven".

'*God*, this brings back memories,' Carla murmured from only inches away, and I wondered if her thoughts had strayed to the same memory as mine. She shifted in the darkness, possibly trying to gain enough space and time to consider if and what she wanted to happen next.

I didn't give her time to decide.

Before she could say anything else, I closed the slight distance between us. She gasped and jumped when I suddenly pressed my body against hers. Blinded by the darkness and her distracting memories, she had not anticipated my approach.

I kissed her. The taste and feel was different than I remembered; her tongue was lethargic, almost hesitant, whereas she used to be the demanding, aggressive partner in our trysts. The change upset me, but I refused to allow myself any feelings of disappointment. Instead, I kissed her harder. Rougher. I tried physically to draw the Carla I remembered out of the Carla in front of me. She resisted my provocations initially, but my teeth on her plump lower lip finally drew a spark of the old heat and fire from her. Carla whispered my name hoarsely with a curse, and her hands tightened around my upper arms. Growling, she shoved me away from her, and for a heartbeat there was a cool rush of air between our bodies, but before I could even begin to voice a protest, she pulled me close again and her swollen lips found mine.

It was a bold, demanding kiss, and my entire body melted under its heat. I moaned like I used to, brazenly and shamelessly, and she responded just as vocally in turn. Her voice was hoarser than when we last did this. I'm not sure if it was from strain, stress, or substances. I could taste cigarettes when she kissed me, as well as the dark, depressing shadow of liquor. I moved my lips from her mouth to her neck and let them reminisce over the softness of her bare skin.

In the dark, her hand slid from my upper arm to my hip. Again, her touch was uncharacteristically and unnervingly tentative. I had always been used to boldness in her loving, and found myself saddened by her loss of confidence. I changed tactics and channelled my gentlest emotions into my kiss and touch as I slowly began to move my hands over her soft, warm flesh, exploring.

She was intimately familiar and, at the same time, a stranger under my hands. The flat planes and firm muscles I had loved in our late adolescence had filled out and transformed into rounded curves and yielding flesh. There was no sharpness left in her body or tongue any more, just as there were no hard edges in her face or smile.

Everything about her seemed to have grown soft in my absence.

The smoothness and thickness of her body brought an unexpected heat to my pussy. Her full breasts heaved with each hitched, expectant breath and I found myself marvelling at this change between us. Before, I had been overweight, inexperienced, and overly eager to please. Now, the submissive one between us had become the confident, controlling force, and the previously dominant partner was uncertain and desperate for direction.

My mounting desire, though, kept my thoughts from wandering too far away from the warm body pressed against mine. Carla was offering no resistance to my curious hands, so I took that as permission to increase my explorations. She was wearing a short-sleeved blouse. I felt for the top button in the dark, but found the task of properly unbuttoning the garment too trying for my patience. Gripping the light fabric, I pulled sharply.

There was an audible rip and then the sound of buttons clattering across the fake hardwood floor echoed in our small hideaway. Carla started to tell me off, but my fingers silenced her as they slid up her belly and over the generous curves of her heavy breasts. I could feel the delicate lace of her bra under my fingertips, and regretted, for a moment, the darkness of our rendezvous place. I wished I could see the voluptuous curves rising and falling under my touch.

Still, there were advantages to playing in the dark as well.

I stripped my shirt off and let it drop onto the floor at my feet. My bare nipples were already stiff and hard; I pressed my heated body shamelessly against hers, as my hands found her again in the darkness.

Sliding my fingertips into the right cup of her bra, I folded the fabric down and let her breast escape from its support. I felt her body tense as my lips found her nipple blindly and latched on, while my other hand dropped down to her cotton skirt and slipped easily between the waistband and her body.

Despite all the changes in Carla's body and behaviour, her reaction as I pushed aside her cotton panties and pressed my fingers against her damp slit was just as I remembered. With a deep, dramatic moan, she arched her back and spread her legs wider, allowing me easy access to both her swollen pussy and hard nipples.

I trailed my fingertips slowly up and down the coarse hair covering her opening, occasionally letting the very tips of my index and middle fingers slip between the lips of her vagina, while my mouth closed around her nipple. Sucking the hardened nub between my teeth, I applied a gentle pressure to the sensitive skin as I continued to tease her lower body with my hand.

She was growing more vocal; one hand was on the back of my neck, alternately gripping my hair and squeezing the nape of my neck to encourage my amorous actions. Her other hand had slid down my back and I could feel her manicured nails beginning to scratch long marks into my skin as my teasing attentions continued to arouse her frustrations.

Over our combined, heavy panting, I noticed the music beyond the door had softened. I could hear Bon Jovi's *Always* crooning over the reminiscent crowd outside. I pictured the couples pressed close and swaying slowly to the bittersweet song. By comparison, though, and in conflict to the calming melody, my body was unbearably aroused and energized.

Taking pity on both her mounting arousal and my own, I bit down suddenly on her captured nipple while my index and middle fingers penetrated her wet, inviting pussy to the knuckle in one slick motion.

She vibrated around my fingers, her cry of pleasure making my own pussy ache for attention. I scissored my fingers inside her, loving the way her muscles gripped and stretched around my exploring digits. At the same time, I pressed my thumb against the top of her slit.

Her grip at the back of my neck had grown painful. Releasing her nipple, I moved my mouth upwards, trailing kisses across the sweaty expanse of skin from her breasts to her neck. Finding her collarbone in the dark, I nipped at the warm flesh, delighting in her gasps of mock pain and genuine pleasure, before her hands caught my face and forced my attention back onto her lips.

Her kiss was hard enough to bruise and I felt my cunt quiver at the harshness of her desire. Pulling my fingers back out of her pussy, I felt her wetness dripping over my knuckles and down the back of my hand. She had never been more wantonly aroused or attractive to me. Pressing my hand against her slit again, I slipped four fingers into her welcoming pussy and, bending my fingers slightly, began to steadily thrust in and out of her damp opening.

She was devouring my mouth as her swollen vaginal muscles contracted and tried to devour my fingers. My free hand found her neglected nipple and began to pinch the hard nub while I increased the pace of my fingers. I was actually beginning to worry I wouldn't be capable of a frantic enough pace to satisfy her ravenous cunt, when her body suddenly tensed, her nails dug sharply into my back, and a stream of raw, desperate pleas began to spill from her lips.

The song came to an end before her climax did; her hoarse cries reached the main room as the music faded out, and within seconds our red-faced hostess was at the closet door. As Leanne pulled it open, a widening beam of light fell across Carla's face, and we stared at one another.

My eyes hungrily roamed over the half-undressed, dishevelled woman before me, trying to memorise every generous curve. Likewise, her eyes were travelling over my bare chest.

'Those are new …,' she purred, nodding towards my tattooed left shoulder. I glanced down at my inked flesh, startled to feel a faint blush heating my face under her attentive, appraising gaze.

'Yeah, I got these right after … us …'

She nodded, letting that explanation hang between us silently, before a seductive grin suddenly crossed her face. 'I'll have to take a closer look at them,' she whispered.

Ignoring both our hostess's scowl and the curious faces peeking over Leanne's shoulders, my ex reached out to grab my belt buckle in one hand and the door knob in the other. Then, with an audacity that echoed the bold spirit of the brash, loud girl I had loved so intensely six years ago, Carla pulled me against her while she slammed the door shut in our friends' gaping faces.

When in Devon
by Lucy Felthouse

Belle was bored out of her damn mind. She sat on a deckchair on Croyde Beach, watching her friends, Adrian and Wayne, surfing. It had been fun at first, seeing their athletic bodies manoeuvring the boards with skill, riding the waves. And giggling at the occasional fall, of course. They were good, but not perfect.

Now, on the third day of walking from their lush holiday cottage to the beach to watch the surfers, Belle really wished she'd stayed in and taken advantage of the free WiFi. Or even gone into the village pub or café. Read a book. Anything but continue to observe the boys on their bloody boards.

She wasn't even supposed to be there, really. A third guy, Max, was meant to be going, but he'd dropped out for some reason, so the others had asked her if she wanted to come along.

'Come on,' Adrian had said, 'there are three bedrooms, all en suite, so it'll be private for you. Free WiFi, underfloor heating, the works.'

'Sounds expensive.'

'It is, but not for you. Max has already paid his share, and it was non-refundable. We won't find another surfer to come at such short notice, so Max will have to take the hit. He's OK with it. Anyway, you've gotta come. You don't have other plans, do you?'

His voice sounded slightly incredulous at that last part, and Belle's reply was snippy.

'No, I don't. But there's no need to be mean about it.'

'Sorry, babe. I didn't mean it like that. How about I make it up to you? A free week away do you? All you need is spending money.'

'No petrol money? Are we teleporting there?'

'Hey, who's being mean now? Anyway, no you don't. I invited you, and I wouldn't expect you to pay for petrol. Come on …' He wheedled and cajoled.

Belle gave in. She'd only really been stubborn because of the comment about her not having anything else to do. Inwardly, she'd jumped at the chance of a free holiday, but she'd remained cool on the outside.

Now, though, she wished she'd remained cool through and through, or that her boss had refused to give her the time off. Yes, it had been nice to see what her two best friends did every time they tore off to the Devon or Cornwall coast, but now she'd had her fill.

It wasn't all bad, though. The weather was gorgeous, especially for early November, and there was hardly anyone around. She imagined the place would be heaving in the summer, but now there were just a handful of surfers, the occasional dog walker, and a few hikers.

The hikers gave her an idea. She could go for a walk. Take in a bit more of the scenery, something different from the section of beach she'd been staring at for three days straight. Yes, that's what she'd do. Rummaging in the bag she'd brought with her, she found an old receipt and a pen.

Gone for a walk. Got my mobile if you need me. Belle xxx

She found a stone on the beach and used it to weight

the note as she placed it on the deckchair to her left. The boys couldn't possibly miss it – even if they didn't spot it, one of them would sit on it sooner or later, and that stone would *hurt*. She giggled at the thought, half-wishing she could hide somewhere and watch the potential funny thing happen.

Belle was just moving out of her chair when she spotted movement on the beach in front of her. A wetsuit-clad figure had emerged from the sea and was jogging up the beach, carrying a surfboard. Instantly, Belle knew it wasn't Adrian or Wayne. The person was too short, and not nearly wide enough. As they got closer, she spotted curves and realised the figure was female. Whoever she was, she was heading straight for Belle.

She settled back into her seat, and looked around to see if there were any other piles of stuff lying about that the girl might have left and was now returning to. There was nothing. Turning back, she saw the woman had almost reached her, and rearranged her features from a frown into a more welcoming expression. Just because there had been a mix-up, she didn't have to scare her off.

'Hi,' the other girl said as she reached her. She stuck the end of her surfboard into the sand, then flopped into the deckchair beside Belle – fortunately the one without the note and the stone. 'I'm Chloe.'

'H-hi, Chloe.' She took the hand that had been offered to her and shook it. 'I'm Belle.'

'I know.' She grinned, and the effect was startling. Belle had already been thinking that Chloe was a hottie, and now she'd had the belief confirmed, big style.

'Y-you know?' Her frown returned.

'Yeah. I know Adrian and Wayne. And Max too. We've bumped into each other loads of times here. I was chatting to the guys – well, as much as you can chat when

103

you're on a surfboard – and they told me what happened with Max. They also told me all about his replacement, and said it would be OK to grab one of their chairs while I took a break.'

'Oh, OK. Fair enough. It's nice to meet you. But I'm afraid I'll have to leave you to it. I was just going to take a walk.'

'Mind if I come with you?' Chloe scraped her fingers through her wet hair, making the cropped strands stand on end. 'I could do with warming up.'

And I'd like to warm you up, Belle thought. Shoving the idea away, she said, 'Of course. I'm guessing you probably know the area, so we'll know where we're going, rather than me just wandering aimlessly.'

Chloe nodded, then stood up again and started to unzip her suit. Belle bit back a moan as the other girl's body was revealed. She was all toned muscle, but with curves in all the right places. She averted her gaze before Chloe spotted her shameless perving.

'It's all right,' Chloe said, with a grin. 'I've got a bikini on underneath.'

Ha, if only you knew why I'd really turned around. 'Excellent. Well, I'm ready when you are.'

'Yep, OK. Mind if we stop off at my car first so I can get some shoes and drop off my board?'

Belle's gaze dropped to the other girl's bare feet. 'No worries. Is it far? Wouldn't want you getting your feet cut or anything.'

Chloe grinned. 'Aww, thanks. I'll be fine. The car park is only a minute or so away, and it's on the way too.'

'The way to where?'

'Baggy Point.'

'Oh, OK.' Belle stifled a giggle at the daft name – the last thing she wanted was for the hot surfer chick to think she was some kind of immature idiot. Which she was, of course; she just didn't want it to be public knowledge.

'So, let's go.'

With that, Chloe grabbed her drysuit and board made her way up the beach with Belle in tow. Belle couldn't help but look at the girl in front of her; delectable arse wiggling in her tiny bikini, and lovely legs that she imagined would feel good wrapped around her. Suddenly, she felt hot, and not just from the sun.

They stepped onto the road, leaving the sand behind – which Belle was happy about. She found it difficult to walk on and hated getting it in between her toes, though she hadn't noticed it too much this time, what with being distracted by Chloe's hot body and all.

'OK –' Chloe turned to Belle with a smile '– the car park is just up here, then we carry on along this road to get to Baggy Point. This is actually the South West Coast Path.'

'Cool – I had no idea. I've often toyed with the idea of doing a long distance trail walk, but I don't think it's really for me. I like to stop and look at interesting things, take lots of photos and stuff. On a long distance trek, though, I bet the walkers are just eager to get to their final destination for the night before their feet drop off!'

'I know what you mean. Well, since you like looking at things and taking photos, you're going to love where we're going. Have you got your camera?'

'Yep.' She patted her bag, which she'd picked up, pulling the strap over her head as they left the deckchairs.

'Cool.'

With that, they continued in silence along the road. Before long, Belle saw a car park. It seemed to be the one they were aiming for, as when they reached the opening in the wall, Chloe headed through it. She fished her car keys from somewhere – probably a secret pocket in her drysuit or something, Belle thought – and picked her way carefully across the stony surface to a vehicle that was a cross between a car and a van. It wasn't the most attractive mode of transport, but Belle figured it needed to be the size it was to fit the surfboard inside.

Sure enough, Chloe unlocked the back doors of the car-cum-van and slid her board inside, before grabbing a large T-shirt, a pair of socks, and some walking shoes. She pulled the T-shirt over her head. Belle's heart sank a little when she saw just how much of Chloe's figure the thing covered up. Then the other girl sat in the back of the van and pulled the socks on, quickly followed by the shoes. She tied the laces tightly before looking up at Belle with a grin.

'What? We're going to a cliff edge; I don't want to end up falling over and plummeting to my death because I've tripped over my flip-flops.'

Belle looked down at her own flip-flopped feet in horror. 'I don't want to plummet to my death either!'

Chloe stood up and moved towards her. 'You won't. I'll hold on to you. Keep you safe.'

The other girl was so close that Belle could smell the sea – or it could have just been her imagination. Either way, Chloe's proximity was doing funny things to her, not least creating a pleasant warmth between her thighs.

Belle was getting so hot and bothered that she couldn't think of anything to say in reply. So, after a couple of seconds of silence, Chloe shrugged, then reached back into the van for her bag, slammed and locked the doors, and dropped the keys into her bag, which she then slung over her shoulder.

She turned to Belle. 'Coming?'

Belle nodded, and the two of them continued walking

up the road, past self-catering holiday cottages and a café and then out onto the peninsula.

'There's not much else out here, a couple more houses, a farm or two and then just the countryside right to the tip of the peninsula. The whole thing is owned by the National Trust now – some rich family gave it to them years ago.'

'If I had land like this, I'd be selfish and keep it all to myself.'

'I don't blame you.'

They continued walking in silence for a while, until they reached a fork in the road where their path lay to the left, skirting the edge of the cliffs – but fortunately, Belle thought, not too closely.

'Are you all right in those?' Chloe nodded towards Belle's feet. 'They comfy?'

'Yeah, they're fine, thanks. Why?'

'Cos we've got a little way to go, is all. Don't want you getting blisters or anything!'

'I'm OK. Thanks.'

They weren't far along the path before Belle saw something that demanded her attention. 'Oh my God,' she said, picking up speed, 'what's that?'

Chloe didn't respond, knowing she'd find out soon enough.

'Oh wow,' Belle said as she reached the thing that had caught her eye. 'It's a –' she read the sign situated next to it '– whale bone? Wow, really? It looks more like a weirdly shaped rock.'

'I know. It's cool, isn't it?'

'It sure is. Oh, hang on.' She fished in her bag for her camera and took a few shots of the whale bone, before switching the device back off. 'OK, I'm ready. I'm going to keep it handy, though, in case I see any other cool things.'

'Oh don't worry, you will. This place is awesome.'

The two of them shared a smile and continued along the path, past lots of beautiful countryside, fields on one side and dramatic craggy rock faces on the other.

'People do a lot of rock climbing here. Look.' Chloe pointed out a length of brightly coloured rope which was coiled up next to a backpack. 'If you get a bit closer, you'll be able to see them.'

'Er, no, you're all right. I'll take your word for it. I'm keeping my feet firmly on the ground, thank you very much.'

Chloe shrugged. 'Fair enough. We're almost there.'

Belle looked ahead and thought she could see the outcrop they were heading for. 'It's really beautiful here. I love it.' With that, she switched on her camera and fired off a few shots of the surrounding area, including the direction they were headed in. 'This is great. Thanks for bringing me here.'

'You're welcome. Don't use all your battery or your memory, though, there will be lots more photos you'll want to take when we get there.'

'OK.'

They continued in silence for a while longer, then shifted into single file as the land narrowed. Belle trod carefully on the rocky path, paranoid about stepping onto a large stone, losing her balance, and falling down the cliff edge. She was glad that Chloe was in front of her, so she couldn't see what a wimp she was being, placing one foot in front of the other with extreme care, rather than enjoying what was around her.

Soon they were at the end of the path, which had a small grass-covered hump of earth beside it. Belle decided she'd feel more comfortable about checking out the view if she was sitting down, so she did just that.

'Hey,' Chloe said, crouching down and poking her in the arm, 'you've hogged all the space. Make room for a little one.'

Belle looked down at the nearby cliff edge with horror. She didn't want to move any closer to it, no way. She glanced back at Chloe, wide-eyed.

'Oh all right. I've got a better idea.' The surfer chick then walked – with no apparent fear – around the back of Belle and manoeuvred so she was sitting behind her, facing in the same direction and with her legs either side of the other girl's. Belle wasn't sure where Chloe's hands were, but they weren't on her. 'See, you're über-safe now, babe. You're not going anywhere. All right?'

Belle nodded, words eluding her. Probably because she was hyper aware of the fact that Chloe's crotch was right against her bottom, with just a few thin layers of material between them. Fuck.

'Are you OK?' Chloe said, her head appearing beside her own, her chin resting on Belle's shoulder. 'You've gone really quiet.'

'I – I'm OK. Just checking out the scenery.'

'Yeah, me too.' Her tone of voice told Belle that Chloe didn't mean the same scenery she was talking about. She'd suspected the other girl of batting for the same team she did earlier, but couldn't figure out a way of finding out without asking outright, so had kept quiet. Now, her words and the fact she was cuddling up to her confirmed her suspicions.

Belle had no idea what to do next, how to react to the super-sexy girl who was clearly interested in her, so she lifted her camera, switched it on, and took some more photos. She was just zooming in on what she could see of the route they'd taken to get here when two hands slid around her waist, then linked in the middle. Belle tensed momentarily in surprise, then relaxed when her brain caught up with what was going on and she realised that she really didn't mind having the other girl hug her. She couldn't really hug Chloe back, not without twisting her arms into a bizarre and likely very painful position, so she wriggled her body a little, as though shifting happily into the embrace.

Still clicking away on the camera, capturing as much of the surrounding area as she could, she was distracted and therefore utterly surprised when Chloe's wandering hands undid the button and zip of her shorts, then dipped inside. One set of fingers pushed her sweat-dampened labia apart, while the others slipped in between, seeking her clit and pussy. Belle gasped.

'W-what are you doing?'

'What do you think I'm doing? Do you want me to stop?'

'N-no.'

'OK, then I won't.'

'W-what if someone comes?'

Chloe's laugh rang out through the air. 'I'm hoping *you* will, sweet cheeks. But we'll keep an eye out and if anyone *arrives,* I'll have to stop, quick.'

Belle couldn't think of a clever response, so instead she let her body do the talking. She opened her legs, allowing the other girl better access to her crotch.

'Mmm,' came Chloe's voice in her ear, 'you're getting wet so fast. Am I turning you on?'

Belle nodded frantically, clenching her buttocks in order to thrust her pussy into Chloe's hand, urging her on.

'Good. I'm going to make you come, Belle. Question is will you bite your lip and keep quiet, or will you rely on the crashing of the sea and the squawking of the birds to cover up your screams?'

Chloe's words were getting her as hot as the fingers in her knickers were. That was until those fingers began to pinch and stroke at her clit in earnest, finding the particular spot that made her breath come out in short gasps and concentrating on it.

Belle had no idea whether it was the situation or the hot chick, but she felt herself climbing towards climax much more rapidly than she normally did. Her chest heaved and she rested her hands on her thighs, her camera in danger of being broken with the death-grip she was subjecting it to. She wanted to close her eyes, but she was too paranoid that she would miss anyone coming along, and end up being caught with someone else's hands down her pants. So she stared resolutely ahead, her teeth digging harder and harder into her bottom lip as her body was overtaken by pleasure. Just as she worried she was going to taste blood, Chloe picked up her pace on Belle's swollen clit.

'Oh, oh, oh fuck! Carry on like that and I'm going to come!'

'That's kind of the point, babe. Now just relax and let go. I want to feel you come all over my hand.'

The filthy words pushed Belle higher, and soon she felt the tightening of her abdomen that signalled she was teetering on the very edge of climax. A few more strokes from Chloe's skilled fingers and she was forced to bite her fist to muffle her screams as her orgasm hit, hard. Her pussy contracted around Chloe's fingers, pushing out a gush of juices and causing the other girl to gasp.

When Chloe spoke, it was as though Belle was hearing her though a thin wall. 'Wow, that feels amazing.' She pulled her fingers out, and then stuck them in her mouth, sucking off Belle's girl juices. 'Yum. You taste fucking delicious too.' She paused, and Belle heard slurping and sucking sounds. 'That was seriously hot. You OK?'

Belle nodded slowly, her head feeling heavy as she rode out the ebbing waves of her orgasm. 'Mmm-hmm.' She leant back, resting her head on Chloe's shoulder and enjoying the sound of the sea crashing against the cliff base, and the feeling of the sun on her face as she came back to herself.

They sat like that for some minutes, strangely intimate despite the fact they'd only just met. Then Chloe broke the silence. 'Ready to go, sweetheart? Won't the boys be wondering where you've gone?'

'Uh, give me a minute. I don't think my legs are going to work just yet.'

'That good, was it?' Chloe shuffled out from behind Belle and moved around in front of her, hand held out.

'Fuck, yes.' She reached out and took Chloe's hand, allowing the other girl to help her up.

'I'm glad to hear it. How about a repeat performance? My place or yours?' Chloe slung her arm around Belle's waist, pulling her tight against her body for support.

'Whichever's nearest.' Belle grinned, already looking forward to getting Chloe fully naked and returning the blissful orgasmic favour.

'OK, let's go.'

Lesbian Lane
by Lynn Lake

Mindy yelped with glee when the baby-blue convertible pulled over to the side of the highway. She snatched up her backpack and raced over to the open door, jumped inside the car. The driver, a mature, redheaded woman with a full, round face and figure, dressed in a Sunday best blue dress and white stockings, smiled at the 18-year-old and stomped on the accelerator. The car spun out of the gravel and back onto the asphalt.

And only ten miles down the county road, Mindy found out just how friendly the women on this stretch of highway really were, when the driver reached over and slid her right hand into Mindy's green shorts, started rubbing the girl's pussy.

Mindy gulped, gaping down at the woman's hand in her shorts, petting her kitty. 'Um, what are you doing, Celia?' she asked. They'd exchanged names shortly after Mindy had gotten into the vehicle.

'Just making you feel welcome, sweetie,' Celia replied, stroking Mindy's sensitive slit with her fingers. 'You said you were a stranger to this part of the country.'

'Th-that's right,' Mindy gasped. 'I thought I'd, you know, go "on the road" this summer, before I start college in the fall. Try to find myself, I guess.' She grinned nervously, Celia's fingers running through the blonde fur of her pussy faster, petting her puffy lips harder. 'A journey of discovery, if you will. I want to know what I'm all about, you know.'

The irrepressible blonde bunny liked to talk. Almost as much as she liked the way Celia's rubbing fingers made her feel. She leant back against the seat, thrusting out her large breasts in her tight, white T-shirt even more, the rushing wind blowing her long, golden locks around.

'Well, I do hope you find what you're looking for,' Celia said, staring at Mindy's bosomy chest, the girl's long, lush, sunbrowned body. She sunk her shifting fingers into Mindy's juicy pussy lips. 'I know I have.'

Mindy smiled self-consciously. It had all happened so fast, the lovely woman just reaching out and touching her, stroking her. And now Mindy had to admit to herself that she never wanted it to end, Celia's strumming fingers turning her so moist and warm and languid, making her melt right into the car seat. She closed her eyes and sighed. Yes, she wanted *this* ride to go on for ever. This was sure southern hospitality at its finest.

Mindy's eyelashes suddenly batted open, revealing her green cat's eyes again. She looked over at Celia. 'Um, would you mind an awful lot if I took off my top? It's, uh, getting kind of hot in here.'

Celia licked her glossy lips. 'By all means, sweetie.'

It *was* hot, the southern summer sun burning down, bathing everything in sultry yellow heat, the breeze cooling things down not a bit. Mindy pulled her tee up over her head. The wind almost whipped the skimpy, deflated garment right out of her hands, but she hung onto it, dropped it down on the floor of the car. Then she shook out her hair and leant back again, her big breasts starkly bare now.

Mindy's boobs were round and ripe and sunbrowned, white bikini lines highlighting her jutting pink nipples. She felt the swirling air caress her swollen pair, felt Celia's eyes all over them. She slowly slid her slender hands up her flat stomach and under her hanging breasts, cupped and squeezed the sensitive mounds. Two of Celia's fingers plunged right inside Mindy's slit, the woman's thumb buffing the girl's swelled-up clit.

'Oh!' Mindy moaned, closing her eyes again, feeling up her tits, revelling in the wonderful sensations racing through her body as fast as the car down the highway.

'You're a beautiful girl,' Celia breathed, pumping her fingers into Mindy, thumb-polishing her clit, glancing every now and then at the road.

Mindy whimpered. The delicious joy in her was building and building, getting ready to burst. She pinched her throbbing nipples between her long fingers, arching with additional pleasure. Celia's fingers in her pussy pumped deeper, thumb riding her clit even harder. It was too much for Mindy, too much unexpected, utterly wicked stimulation.

'Oh Celia!' the girl wailed. 'I'm – I'm …'

Mindy exploded with passionate feeling, hot, blissful orgasm welling up around Celia's pistoning fingers, under Celia's buffing thumb, and tidal-waving through her young body. She thrust her pussy up into the erotic storm, squeezing her breasts so hard the nipples were in danger of shooting off. She rolled her blonde head from side to side on the back of the seat, transported to a place of pure heated contentment.

Celia pulled her fingers out of Mindy's pussy when the girl at last stopped spasming. Then she stuck them into her own mouth, and urgently sucked up Mindy's sticky, ecstatic juices, swallowed them down.

'They keep me young!' she gasped at the startled girl, excitedly tonguing her fingers to get every last drop.

'Oh OK,' Mindy agreed. She'd heard of some strange beauty treatments before, but this took the cake.

Celia pulled off the road and let Mindy out of the car, once her fingers had been licked clean.

Mindy didn't have to wait long for another ride. She stuck out her thumb and cocked her hips, bending one long, bronze leg and thrusting her chest out. A pick-up truck slewed off the highway and skidded to a stop on the shoulder up ahead. Mindy ran for the open door.

There were two women in this vehicle. 'Hi, I'm Chantelle!' the one behind the wheel introduced herself. 'And this is my sister-in-law, Clarisa,' she added, nodding at the woman next to her.

'Mindy!' Mindy yelped.

The girl jumped into the red pick-up when Clarisa slid over on the bench seat to make room. She looked at the two women. They actually looked more like sisters than sisters-in-law. They both had short, black hair cut into bangs, large violet eyes, plush red lips, and button noses. They were both wearing tight pink halter tops and cut-off blue jean shorts. Their skin was the colour and texture of alabaster, their breasts small with pointed nipples.

'Where you headed?' Chantelle asked, turning the truck back onto the road and quickly picking up speed.

'That's what I'm trying to find out,' Mindy stated honestly. 'Um, if you know what I mean.'

The two women exchanged glances, then chimed together, 'We know exactly what you mean!'

Mindy grinned.

It was a tight fit in the small pick-up, Clarisa's bare arm pressing into Mindy's. But then it got even tighter, closer, barer, when Clarisa suddenly slid forward off the seat and down onto her knees on the floor of the truck. She shifted over in between Mindy's legs, spread the girl's long, supple pair.

'I've found what I'm looking for,' she said, looking up into Mindy's startled eyes.

'And I like to watch,' Chantelle added.

Before Mindy could even comprehend what exactly was happening, Clarisa had pulled Mindy's shorts down and plunged her tongue into the girl's pussy. Mindy jumped and squealed, the other woman's tongue hitting home, scoring a bullseye between her lips.

'Lick her! Lick her sweet cunt!' Chantelle urged, clutching the steering wheel with whitened knuckles, her sandaled foot tromping down on the accelerator.

Clarisa gripped Mindy's quivering thighs and bobbed her head in between Mindy's legs, bangs flying, slurping excitedly at Mindy's steamy blonde pussy. Mindy gripped the arm rest on one side, Chantelle's proffered hand on the other, Clarisa's tongue painting her slit and shooting her full of tingling sensation. Every strong, budded lap the woman gave her sent her pelvis arching upwards, her body flooding with shimmering heat. The road blurred in front of her eyes, Clarisa's wicked tongue-stroking blinding her to everything but her surging emotions.

Clarisa writhed her tongue almost right around to Mindy's bumhole, then licked upward with a powerful dragging stroke, all the way up to Mindy's blossomed clit. She licked over and over and over, lapping faster and harder. Mindy's juices tasted sweet and tangy on the end of her tongue, the girl's pussy lips engorged and wrinkly textured. She reached up and shot her hands under Mindy's T-shirt, grabbed onto the girl's large breasts.

'Oh my!' Mindy shrieked. She'd never felt anything like it. The intimate licking beat even Celia's intimate petting, any variation of self-pleasure Mindy had invented for herself back home.

She twisted her head over to stare at Chantelle. That woman grinned at her, gripping her hand. Mindy wasn't sure who was driving the truck any more.

Chantelle husked, 'Eat her out, Clarisa! Stick your tongue inside her wet, delicious pussy and eat her out!'

Mindy gaped at the woman, down at Clarisa. That woman had stopped licking, was looking up at Mindy as she washed her long, pink tongue over her glistening lips. Mindy braced herself for what was going to happen next. But it still shocked and thrilled her when Clarisa pulled her flaps apart and shot tongue right into Mindy's pussy.

'Ohmigod!' Mindy cried, shuddering with pleasure. Clarisa's tongue surged deep into her pink, just as deep as a pair of fingers.

Clarisa twisted her tongue around inside Mindy's pussy, her nose pressing against the girl's clit, her eyes glaring up into Mindy's flashing eyes. She pumped back and forth, fucking Mindy with her licker, Mindy's pink, wet tunnel squeezing tight. All the time, Clarisa gripped and groped Mindy's boobs, plucked at the girl's pointed nipples.

'Suck her clit!' Chantelle yelled. 'Suck on her clit until she comes in your face, Clarisa!'

Mindy's eyes shot wide open. Her clit was a hard, pink button, throbbing against Clarisa's nose. It couldn't take any more stimulation without exploding with passion.

Mindy felt Clarisa's tongue slowly snake out of her slit, leaving her gapingly, pantingly empty. The woman took one long, last lick at Mindy's brimming pussy, then smiled, popped up Mindy's cute pink clit with her fingers and flowed her sticky lips around it, sealed tight.

Mindy vibrated, her breasts jumping in Clarisa's grip, her fingernails biting into Chantelle's clutching hand. Clarisa sucked on Mindy's trigger, her cheeks billowing with the wickedly applied erotic pressure. And Mindy went sailing, shooting up to the fluffy clouds high in the sky, propelled heavenward by the detonation of utter ecstasy in her clit between Clarisa's vaccing lips.

Clarisa took the hot squirts of orgasm all over her chin, washing her face in it, her mouth never letting up on Mindy's pulsating clit.

When the girl landed back down on Earth again, Clarisa and Chantelle helped Mindy out of the truck by the side of the road. 'My turn next time,' Mindy vaguely heard Chantelle remark to Clarisa, before the two women sped off.

Mindy staggered out of the hot sun and into an air-conditioned truck stop a short distance up the highway. But if she'd thought things were going to cool down any, she was happily mistaken.

'Well, well, if isn't Miss Titty Sunshine,' a woman remarked, when Mindy entered the little girls' room to freshen up.

'Yeah,' the other woman with her commented, pulling a cigarette out of her mouth.

The two women were leaning up against the sinks, looking tough in their plaid work shirts with the arms ripped out, their torn blue jeans and scuffed work boots. With their hair cut short and no make-up on their faces.

But they didn't frighten Mindy. She was way beyond mellow.

'Hi!' she bubbled, waving at the women and walking over to a stall, her boobs bouncing and her smile buoyant.

The taller of the two women, a lean girl with spiky black hair and smouldering dark eyes, olive skin all adorned with tattoos, threw down the toothpick she'd been chewing on and said, 'Look at that, would you? Miss Sunshine Booby thinks she can charm us like all those grease monkeys out in the restaurant.'

The other woman's hair was dyed a striking purple. She was shorter and plumper, with big brown eyes and caramel skin, plenty of piercings. 'As if,' she puffed between smoke rings.

They walked up to Mindy, grabbed one of the girl's shoulders each and rubbed.

'I'm Stella,' the taller one said. 'You think you're something pretty special, huh?' She ran her hand up and down Mindy's bare arm.

'Lucita,' the other woman introduced herself. 'Yeah, a real charmer.' Her hand slid off Mindy's shoulder and onto Mindy's chest, swirled around there.

'We're all special – in our own way,' Mindy chirped, never expecting such a warm welcome in the women's washroom of a truck stop. 'I'm Mindy!'

The women's hands slid down under Mindy's breasts, cupped and squeezed the full, firm flesh through the girl's tee. Mindy sighed, her chest and boobs shimmering all over again, her pussy moistening. The women hooked their fingers into Mindy's T-shirt and pulled the flimsy garment right up over the blonde's head. Mindy's bared boobs popped out into the open, fleshy masses quivering, nipples swelling up rapidly.

Stella and Lucita breathed hard, staring at the girl's luscious breasts.

'A real blonde sugar pie,' Stella breathed, licking her lips.

'Yeah,' Lucita murmured, the cigarette dropping out of her mouth, her bright pink tongue sliding over her plush lips.

Mindy grinned at the two women, thrusting her chest out even more, happy to oblige. They clutched her boobs, looked at one another, then latched their lips onto Mindy's jutting nipples and sucked hard.

Mindy moaned, shivering. Stella and Lucita squeezed Mindy's breasts with their warm, kneading hands and slapped her nipples with their strong, flailing tongues, pulled on Mindy's tits with their wet, hungry mouths, dousing the girl's heaving chest and body in good feeling.

Then Lucita dropped Mindy's one boob and dropped down to her knees on the floor, dragging Mindy's shorts along with her. She pushed the girl's long legs apart and stuck out her tongue and slurped Mindy's blonde pussy, making Mindy jump. Stella caught up both of Mindy's quivering breasts and groped them, mashed her mouth against Mindy's, thrust her wet tongue inside.

Mindy blazed with pure pleasure, her nipples humming and pussy juicing.

Until an older lady suddenly walked in on them, looking to use the washroom too.

Stella and Lucita quickly pulled Mindy over to one of the stalls, then pulled her inside. They sat the breathless girl down on the black toilet seat and stripped off their work shirts and jeans. Neither of them was wearing any underwear at all.

Stella stood up on the toilet seat, planting her feet on either side of Mindy's thighs. She pressed her hands against the tiled wall and her pussy into Mindy's face. The blonde bunny gasped, guessing what the woman wanted her to do. And after only a moment's hesitation, she did it, though she'd never done it before. She grabbed onto Stella's hard little bum cheeks and thrust out her tongue and licked all the way up Stella's shaven slit.

The woman spasmed and groaned, getting exactly what she wanted, grabbing Mindy's head and splatting the girl's face even deeper into her wet pussy. Mindy lapped like a kitten at a cream dish, instinctively, naturally, hungrily.

Lucita went down on her knees, in between Mindy's legs again. Mindy felt the woman's hot hands grasp her thighs, the woman's even hotter tongue swab her pussy. She shuddered like Stella was shuddering in her face, giving licks and getting licked.

Until the standing woman suddenly flooded Mindy's mouth with her hot, happy juices. Then Stella took Lucita's place at Mindy's pussy, while Lucita offered her dark-furred pussy up to Mindy on the toilet.

Mindy grasped Lucita's bigger butt cheeks and swiped the woman's thick pussy lips with her tongue. Stella pulled Mindy's flaps apart and wrapped her lips right around the girl's pink button. Mindy cried out into Lucita's pussy, gushing sweet joy into Stella's mouth.

Everyone got off on the good gooey times, even the older lady in the stall next door, by the sounds of it. Mindy marvelled at the wonder of it all.

Mindy had only just stepped out of the truck stop and back onto the side of the highway when a mini-van screeched to a halt up ahead, smoked its tyres backing up to Mindy. The sliding door of the green van slid open and a woman popped her head out and said, 'Looking for a ride?'

'Yes!' Mindy responded eagerly. The women *sure* were friendly on this stretch of road. She climbed into the mini-van and plopped down on the rear bench seat, rocked back as the van took off.

There was a raven-haired girl of about Mindy's age at the wheel. Her name was Catherine. While seated next to Mindy on the rear seat were two older women, one with fluffy blonde hair and blue eyes and tanned skin, the other with black curly hair and big brown eyes and dark skin. They were Tamara and Lashonda, respectively.

Introductions complete, Tamara remarked, 'Catherine just got her driver's licence, so we're letting her drive.' The long, lean, attractive woman elbowed Lashonda next to her. 'Riding's more fun, anyway.'

Lashonda smiled brilliant white teeth and nodded her head, looking at Mindy. She was short and somewhat plump, with large breasts and bottom, dressed in a short purple dress that left none of her assets to the imagination. Tamara was wearing just a thin yellow sundress.

Mindy grinned at the women, her own large breasts jostling under her T-shirt as they bounced over a bump in the road. 'Oh, I like to ride too!'

'And be ridden?' Tamara asked, placing a long, slender hand on Mindy's bare thigh.

'Come again?'

'We sincerely hope so,' Lashonda quipped.

Tamara leant closer and kissed Mindy on the lips, a long, soft, wet kiss that left the girl's head dizzy and her breasts and pussy dazzled. The atmosphere of the van was heavy and lush with the scent of the women's perfume. Mindy quickly got the idea that this was going to be one sweet ride, as well.

And sure enough, in no time at all, the three women in the backseat were out of their clothes and naked as the day. Mindy had lost a lot of her inhibitions already in her recent travels, but she was still glad that the mini-van sported tinted windows, so fellow travellers couldn't peek in and see what naughtiness the trio of women were up to. Although, that actually would be kind of exciting too, Mindy realised.

But the excitement was already coming at her fast and fantastic, from both sides. She was in the middle now, Tamara on her right, Lashonda on her left. The women took turns kissing her, tonguing her wantonly outstretched tongue. Mindy's head spun even more, inside and out, two beautiful women sensuously kissing her again, petting her bare breasts, playing with her rigid nipples.

Then the women both bent their heads lower and lifted Mindy's young breasts up to their mouths, twirled their pink tongues around Mindy's nipples, lighting up the girl's body even more. She quivered with joy, the women sucking her engorged nipples into their mouths and tugging on them.

'Oh my, yes!' Mindy gulped, staring at Catherine behind the wheel.

The young woman's shoulder was moving, like she was rubbing her pussy as she drove, her head turned to see what was going on in the backseat. Until the roar of a big rig brushing by made her take in the sexy action from the relative safety of the rear-view mirror.

Tamara and Lashonda sucked hard, lustily on Mindy's nipples, nipping at the buzzing pink tips with their teeth, stretching the jutters back to Mindy's squirming delight. Then the two women released Mindy's breasts and nipples and climbed onto the seat on either side of her on their knees. They cupped and thrust their breasts into Mindy's face, smiling down at the flustered blonde.

Mindy had never licked, sucked another woman's boobs before. Yes, she'd pushed up her own big breasts and tongued the tips, tugged on them with her lips, in the midst of some private fantasies in her own bedroom. But this was something completely different.

Mindy happily grasped Lashonda's huge, chocolate boobs and flailed the woman's liquorice nipples with her tongue. She'd already gotten so much on this road trip, it was time to give some back.

Lashonda's thick nipples swelled even further under Mindy's thrashing tongue. The young woman eagerly poured her lips over one and sucked on it; did the same to the other. And she was obviously doing something right, despite her inexperience, because Lashonda moaned and gripped Mindy's windblown blonde hair.

Mindy unhanded and unmouthed Lashonda's breasts and nipples, turned her head, excitedly painted Tamara's tan nipples with her tongue. Then she sucked on Tamara's smaller, but firmer, breasts. She bobbed her head back and forth, gripping and groping heated tit-flesh, gorging on her rubbery nipple. She couldn't get enough, her hunger for women unleashed.

Finally, however, Mindy found herself positioned on all fours on the backseat of the van. Tamara was behind, up on her knees, Lashonda stretched out in front with her legs open. Tamara had strapped on a black dildo that Catherine had handed back to the woman.

Mindy felt the silicon dong gently whack her upraised bum cheeks as she stared into Lashonda's dark, wrinkly, glistening pussy lips. She wasn't totally sure what was going to happen next, what she was expected to do. The van sailed down the highway, and the two kind, knowledgeable women showed Mindy the way.

Tamara speared the strapped-on dildo into Mindy's dripping pussy, right to the hilt, as Lashonda grasped Mindy's blonde head and splatted the girl's face in between her legs. Mindy gasped as the dildo sunk home into her pink tunnel, gulped in the face of Lashonda's wet pussy.

Mindy grasped Lashonda's fleshy thighs and tongued her steamy twat as Tamara rocked her from behind, thrusting the dong back and forth in her own pussy.

Lashonda tasted wonderful, tangy and spicy. Mindy dragged her tongue over the woman's puffy lips and swollen clit again and again, revelling in the feel, the texture, the scent, the spasms of joy she was eliciting from her. Spurred on by Tamara's pumping dildo in her slit.

'Fuck her, Tamara!' Catherine cried from the front of the van, her glaring grey eyes locked on the mirror. 'Lick her, Mindy!'

They didn't need any encouragement. Mindy lapped, Tamara pumped, Lashonda groaned.

Tamara's fingers bit into Mindy's waist as she thrust faster, harder, full length into the girl. The leather platform of the dildo-mount squished against her own pussy with every pump, setting her clit to buzzing wildly. She gritted her teeth, her face set, her breasts shuddering, her thighs smacking against Mindy's rippling bum.

Lashonda laced her fingers into Mindy's hair and thrust her pussy into Mindy's face. Her breasts ballooned out obscenely between her squeezing arms, jutting nipples shining with Mindy's saliva. She shivered with each wet, warm stroke of Mindy's tongue, the girl making her pussy smoulder and body shimmer.

Mindy lapped like a madwoman, painting Lashonda's pussy with her tongue, slurping up the woman's hot, leaking juices. Her own pussy burned with the stoking action of Tamara fucking her.

She thrilled with the wicked lesbian loving, pushing her bum back to meet Tamara's banging, pushing her head forward to consume Lashonda's pussy. She saw stars, felt heaven, orgasm enveloping her in its warm, wonderful, gripping arms – a woman's arms.

Lashonda screamed and bucked, bathing Mindy's face in her pussy juices. Tamara groaned and jerked, coating the dildo platform with her ecstatic ejaculate, driving the dong as deep as it would go in Mindy's spasming pussy.

'I think my journey of self-discovery is complete,' Mindy declared to all three women afterwards. 'I am most definitely a lesbian!'

The women smiled. Tamara and Lashonda hugged Mindy, welcoming the girl into the pink fold.

'It's a good thing you are too,' Catherine remarked, glancing at the grinning blonde in the backseat. 'Because this stretch of highway between Potterston and Ames City is known as "Lesbian Lane", a pick-up alley for girls who like girls.'

That was news to Mindy. She thought for a moment, then blurted, 'Looks like I've been travelling the right road all along!'

Pleasing Claudea
by Jayne Wheatley

As a wave of late summer air brushed against my skin, I shivered as though in protest to what I was doing. My neck prickled in anticipation. My feet were scratching the dusty ground with each tired step I took, and fear was gripping inside my body. Besides the long sea voyage this was the most afraid I'd been. No one had spoken to me, only occasionally passing me wine and water to drink and bread to eat. And now through the narrow streets I shuffled, held tight by a man behind as if I would escape in this unfamiliar city. The words they spoke I could not understand, and the deeper into the city we got, the more people lined the streets. There was laughter, excitement, and people all trying to get a view of me. I felt on display, like a prized animal led to its slaughter.

I had been dressed in suitable robes, wrapped around me much like all the other women, but I knew I was different. I had been plucked from my own settlement, chosen especially to represent my people to the emperor. I was not sure what to expect, but a sparkle of excited tension passed through me, making the fear peak once more. I could see hills topped in temples and olive trees sprawled out behind. It looked enviably calmer up away from this bustle now ahead of me.

Even as my legs seemed to want to give way beneath me, I was ushered still forward into a big, open square. People had gathered in several crowds and we wound a path through them, yet as we reached some stairs, I was pulled down to my knees by the man who had up to this point been pulling me along; not roughly, but the action surprised me and I let out an involuntary shriek. Upon the high stairs, a very fine woman laughed behind her hands. I looked up to her fully, taking in the image of her curves under her own cream robes. She looked back, aghast that I would dare initiate contact, her sharp but beautiful features accentuated in her disdainful glare. A warming glow radiated from my loins, a moistness forming as I realised how I could affect the lovely woman.

From somewhere within one of the columned buildings – such wealth as I'd never seen – a low horn sounded, and immediately everyone dropped to their knees. A silence fell among the masses, and I followed their example by bowing my head. A breeze whipped up dust from the ground as a voice spoke, foreign words to me, but the crowd cheered loudly. I chanced a look up, and found the sight of the dark, bronzed man a little overwhelming as his presence preceded him. His robes were of the purest white, and upon his head lay a band of golden leaves. He raised a hand, speaking more words to the people around me now rising from their knees. I followed suit, and as I did his gaze fell upon me. A simple flick of his head in itself had ordered me to go up to join him. I trembled in fear, understanding who he was all the more clearly once I'd been able to count the rings laden on his short fingers. Breath seemed to fail me as I stood before him, bowing my head in a mixture of respect and fear. Beside him, another man stood, though not so elegant in dress. I jumped a little in surprise as the new addition turned to me and spoke my own tongue.

'You are welcomed to Rome,' he told me, then repeated it in his own language just after. This courtesy of translation melted my fears away. He carried on, 'I must introduce you to the people. I am Gaius, ambassador to your isles. What is your name? Please, tell us all.'

'Breanna,' I called out in reply, noticing the fine woman again staring directly at me. My stomach rolled in a wave of fresh excitement. Gaius took my hand, pulling me gently towards the other man and placing my hand within his.

'Very well, Breanna. This is the Emperor of Rome …'

Though I had realised who he was, to show the adoration expected of me I gasped audibly, leaning to kiss the largest ring on his hand. His near-black eyes shone, and a wide smile stretched his tanned face.

'Thank you for receiving me so well; I will try and be happy and prosperous here,' I said loudly, Gaius repeating my words so they would understand. The crowd cheered, many hands clapping in approval.

Gaius continued to explain. 'As you know, you are here to negotiate terms of your people with the Emperor. However, you may settle into Rome until such time you are received by him. Claudea will look after you for now.'

As soft fingers touched my elbow, a shudder passed through me. Claudea was the fine woman who had been so intent on seeing how I reacted, and who had scowled at me for so much as looking to her. Gaius's chatter to the crowd had them beginning to disperse, and as Claudea led me away from the Emperor it was hard to work out whether I was still afraid or full of nervous lust for her.

Servants had lifted my bag from my shoulders, taking it to where I assumed I would sleep, and now they followed us into a large building separated from the forum by a series of narrow streets. Steam issued from the entrance, and my breath caught in my chest at this sudden extra layer of heat. The sun had been relentless, feeling like it burnt at my skin, and yet in here it was even hotter. The first chamber was bare, its cool marble floor a welcome respite for my sore feet. Claudea stopped, exchanged some words with the servant, and then left me in the room.

I smiled at him, an olive-skinned boy of around 18 years. His eyes flickered away from my own and he reached forward to touch my shoulder. I flinched, my senses so alive that the briefest motion sent a tingle over my skin. A knot of tension built up in my waist as his deft fingers pulled at the pin securing my robes across my shoulder. With the silver pin removed, the robes nearly fell from me with no persuasion. The servant boy unwrapped me, spinning the fabric into a neat bundle and leaving me completely bare. I shivered in spite of the steam curling out from the next room, somewhat unsure of being so very naked in a place I did not know. The servant boy's eyes cast over my flesh, redness forming across my chest from the heat. He touched it gently, asking a question I could not understand. When he pretended to wince in pain, I understood his thinking that my skin had burnt. I shook my head, and fanned my face with my hands in an attempt to convey the message. He raised his hand a moment, then backed out of the room. I looked around at the pictures high on the walls, wrapping my arms around myself.

He returned very quickly, clutching a small stone jar which he passed to me. I smelt the contents, the scent reminding me of summer flowers and oil. I looked curiously at him, and he mimed rubbing his skin. I nodded in understanding, thanking him in my own tongue. Following his lead, I stepped forth into the next room, which housed a small pool built into the floor against the far wall, and a pile of soft linens on a low table. He gestured towards the pool with one hand and, without any idea what else I could do, I stepped down into the warm water. Much to my surprise the servant boy joined me, as if it were very normal to do so. Sitting down on the bottom, the water reached only my neck, and I concluded this was a bath meant to be sat in. I let my eyes drift shut and the water lapped around me, taking the pains of travelling away as his hands rubbed across my body. He paused across my breasts, sucking in his breath and causing me to do the same. In my mind's eye Claudea was the one touching me so eagerly.

Fresh foaming soaps and the fragrant sunburn oil were massaged into every inch of my skin, and as he travelled up my inner thigh I forgot myself entirely and moaned aloud. A satisfied look crossed his face, and he stepped out of the bath, the robes around him barely concealing excitement for me. Though impressed at his readiness, my lust was building for her and not him. But the attention to my body was provoking an irresistible ache within me. I sighed heavily, getting up out of the pool. Noticing I was shaking, he pulled some of the linen sheets and dried off my skin somewhat, so that the wettest part of myself was deep between my legs. My long red hair had darkened in the water, and began to curl up as it was rubbed dry. He took one final look over me, nodded in approval, and took my hand.

Once again I was led into another room, this time clean, fresh, and in total longing. This central focus of this room was a huge bath which steamed madly. Claudea was lounging within it, her head resting on the edge and her dark hair fanned out behind her. They spoke a few words, and then the servant boy bowed to me, and exited the room. Claudea sat up, narrowing her eyes but smiling as she did. With a long, elegant hand she beckoned me towards her and, as if hooked, I padded my way across to the deep bath. She was sitting on a purposeful ledge; as I gently climbed in – aware that my now tingling body was so exposed to her gaze – I realised the full depth of this pool. I stood formally in its centre, the water slapping at my breasts, causing my nipples to harden. Claudea's eyes passed over me. Her full lips pouted a little as a smile crossed her face, her eyes seeming to darken. I covered my mound with my hands, suddenly afraid of the power she could possess, and reminding myself I was above the rank of a servant. Back home, I had once been promised to the chief of another tribe, which gave me a glowing pride in my looks.

My toes scratched at the stones at the bottom of the pool as I took a testing step her way. She stood up, stepping towards me. My heart beat so very quickly I felt it even thudding within my loins. She too was naked, her large bosom and curved thighs making me wish to run my mouth all over her body. Her deep red nipples eager to be teased, I could not help but stare. Her skin, for a Roman woman, was pale, but smooth as silk and completely unblemished. It was in real contrast to my sun-kissed nose and bosom, though I was not freckled like some of my tribe. With a heaving chest, I bowed politely to her, my hair draping into the overly warm water. She reached out and touched my chin, pulling me up and brushing my hair in one swift motion so it sat on one shoulder. Her touch sent new shudders through me, and she lingered on my hair, gathering it in her hands.

'Ignis,' she whispered, clearly captivated by me. I used

the moment to examine her more closely. Her fingers were long and the nails coated in a deep red paint. It seemed almost as if everything about her was made to cause a wild longing such as I now felt coursing through me. Her stomach was more curved than my own, but her whole body flowed in such a beautiful way that I had to stop myself from reaching out and caressing her that very moment. The sight of her sex was concealed by the water yet I tried to steal a glance. She caught me looking her over and laughed a little. I took the happy look off my face, almost afraid again, though in truth my whole body felt like it was pulsing in need for her attention. As her hand travelled to the back of my neck I could not suppress a tiny gasp at the feeling it stirred. She pulled me in close, and I could feel her ragged breath on my cheek. This close, her eyes were an amber brown shade and full of excitement. I held in a soft moan, and licked my lips in hope she would want to kiss them.

Though she seemed to restrain herself admirably, she was now using both hands to hold me in close to her face. Her dark curls tickled my neck and the warmth spreading from her was almost raging. Yet all at once she gave in, her plumped lips meeting mine in a moment of pure fire. I responded, almost forcefully kissing her back, my tongue tasting her ever so slightly as I teased her lips. My breasts pushed against hers, a jolt of desire pushing deep into my nether mouth as our nipples brushed each other. She moaned into my mouth, and I revelled in knowing I had her as excited as she had me. Had I not been in water she would have seen the lust dripping from me. She was hungry, pushing hard against me as we broke apart, then came back together, mouths passionately locked. As her tongue dipped into my mouth I tasted a sweet wine. It was addictive and I did not want to prise myself from her, so wound my hands around her waist, her hips now rubbing against mine.

She murmured some words I did not understand as we broke apart, then began to nibble her lip as she watched me shaking in front of her. I was sure what she wanted of me but I was too nervous to do anything which might displease her. All I could want in this moment was to serve her, betraying myself in every way. She stepped back once, pulling me along with her, and I leant in to kiss her silken neck. A small cry came from her, and I stopped caring about anything but hearing her in pleasure. As she climbed up out of the pool and sat upon the tiled edge, her long legs dangled into the water and I was able to see her naked thighs. Inside me, everything ached to touch her, and I was drawn in as she settled herself on the side.

She perched there, spreading her creamy legs apart and revealing her sex to me. The intention was clear, and I lowered myself to her hips. Her eyes beckoned me on. I laid my hands down, one on each thigh. The scent of her wet sex filled the air and I couldn't help but kiss her skin, her thigh at first, then working up with soft kisses across her stomach and hipbones. A stifled sound issued from her throat and she threw her head back in longing as I neared the crux of her desire. Her lower lips were a vivid pink, and open to me as though begging for my tongue or hand to touch. I took deft licks, lower and lower, pausing as she held her breath. I wanted her to plead for me, and surely enough she did, and even though I did not understand her words, she pleaded for more with her whole body. Still I teased her. I ran my tongue over her lust, the pinnacle of nerves all clustered in one exquisite hub of flesh. But I barely moved around it; instead, I tensed my mouth around her glistening hole, allowing my tongue to dip down into her. Above me, she squealed in pure delight at the feeling, wrapping her legs around my head to draw me in deeper. I resisted as much as I dared, her musky juices flowing freely over my face as I delved in and out.

Her hands wound in my hair, her moans louder now. Desire and longing crept in every part of my body as I tasted her, my arms shaking as I supported her legs around my shoulders. Her nails dug into the back of my neck, and I stopped, laughing at the power I now possessed. But, determined to please her, I soon returned my licks to her delicate bud. I pressed my tongue down, biting the tight little clit just enough to make her cry in near enough pain. She began to thrash around me, her thighs quivering madly as I continued to chew and suck on her. With each motion of mine, her body became more and more tense. It was as though I had to wind her to breaking point, and I relished in doing so. My own sex burnt in my own longing for her, the pleasing of this divine lady arousing me more highly than any man could.

I reached up to her heaving chest, tweaking her nipple and adding another layer to the wildness of her writhing around me. Each time she climbed towards the peak of her pleasure, I eased myself away from her a little, making her cry out in frustration, though I knew it would be worth it. I assaulted her senses as long as I could bear, enjoying her taste so greatly I wished never to stop. But soon the persuasion of my mouth was too much, and her thighs tightened around me. She screamed in pleasure, sweet juices flooding my mouth as she came above me. As she cried and sobbed I refused to stop, prolonging her bittersweet agony as her body released all its tension.

It seemed as though I had shattered her nerves, and she pulled my head back, kissing my lips, still covered in her juices. Her soft moans became gentler and her eyes had changed, appearing almost catlike. It was very evident that I had pleased her, and as I licked my lips I could still taste her on them. The strength of my own desire was now intense, especially after seeing her in such rapture for me. With a soft push, she sat me down on the ledge so that I was neck deep in the bath. Then she joined me, sitting to my right and leaning in close. I gripped the stone by my legs, needing to calm myself. She whispered strange words to my ear, her breath brushing the skin around my hairline. She teased my hair again and I let my eyes shut in a haze of longing. Every single breath I took was a fresh shiver passing through me and I felt her long fingers grip my knee under the water. Her nails scraped their way up the highly sensitive skin of my thigh, pausing at the crease where leg met hip. I hissed rather than breathed, and she kissed me hard, urgently even.

I opened my eyes to see her looking very satisfied with herself. Something in me wanted to grab her face and push it down on me to lick me like I had with her. But I could not move, and she further rooted me to the spot by extending her hand to touch my sex. I clutched her waist, urging her onward as she found my own sweet spot, circling it with those, long graceful fingers. I was so deeply excited every simple touch put waves of pleasure curling through my body, insistent. I was determined to not succumb to it, but she tried quite without mercy to bring me apart for her amusement. I nearly sobbed as her hand reached back, slipping two fingers deep inside my core. She stopped a moment, waiting for my reaction, and I cried out to her, desperate for more now. As she began a pounding rhythm, all sense and reason left my body. I felt myself weaken into her as she hit such ecstatic points with her fingertips, sliding effortlessly in and out of me.

She was working me in no way I had felt before, each movement nearly pushing me over that edge of lust. It became a fight of wills, her driving into me and me resisting every urge in my body. Her soft fingers felt nothing like the tool of a man; she was able to rub each spot that made me crazed. And she did. I was powerless to her pleasing. It built and built within me, so that I even fought myself to hold back. But it was useless; I whimpered and cried to her as the sensation took me, crashing into climactic bliss. My body shook violently, washes of pure beauty pulling me along with it. My breath came in short gasps and she kissed my mouth once again, gently leading me down from the peak. I was still shaking as she looked deep into my eyes, and I did not suppress a grin.

I must have quite forgotten myself, perhaps even slept, for as I came to, I was laid back on the tiles. Water still lapped about my waist. I jumped, suddenly alert to my nakedness and surroundings. Claudea was nowhere to be seen, yet the contented ripples between my legs told me I had not dreamt of her. I swam in the water to awaken myself, and then climbed out of the pool, my feet slapping down on the marbled floor. It was not cold, but I wrapped my arms around myself, wondering for some time what I should do next. I moved to the door, looking out through the bath house to the street, the people outside going about their lives as usual. It struck me just how different my life would become. A voice stunned me.

'Breanna? Are you quite well?' The voice belonged to Gaius, the words clear to my ears. He stepped into the room, and did not even blush at my nakedness. I nodded, forgetting I could speak.

'Are you cold? Here ...' He offered me some fresh linen, which I took and began to dry my skin. He carried on, 'Is Claudea pleased? She is eager for young, beautiful women, I am told. And wild …'

Now I flushed, failing to suppress a smile as I looked to the floor.

'Yes, she was well pleased, I hope. And I am too. She is like fire, I think,' I told him, and he laughed lightly.

'Are you aware that that is why you have come here?' he asked, leaving me bewildered.

'No, I am here as an envoy, to agree terms of my people with the Emperor, no?'

'Yes, that is your ultimate purpose, Breanna. But how? Did you not think to ask why you were placed in a bath with the Emperor's wife the moment you arrived?'

'The … Emperor's …wife.' Sudden understanding hit me. Of course, it was no accident that she had wanted pleasing; it was no welcome gift to myself. This was my purpose. I could not argue with the prospect.

'Yes, his wife. You were brought to see if you pleased her well. And I expect now they will want you to remain in Rome …' he explained, laying some fresh linen around my shoulders to protect me from chills.

'So, now I have pleased her, the Emperor will request me to stay within his family, and treat my people back home the way we asked?'

'Exactly. And can you really say no to being here?'

I thought about it carefully as he left me. I looked at the smiles of contentment on people's faces outside, the bright sunshine casting down between the buildings and the buzz of the busy city so far from my home. Perhaps I would miss it? Then the memory of tasting Claudea's sweet lips came to me and I smirked to myself, sure that I would be happy here from now on. Peace negotiator or pleasure slave, I was already a part of Rome.

Sweet Hart
by Giselle Renarde

I never slept with Jameson Hart.

My mom thought he was my boyfriend because he was the only guy who ever walked me home. Maybe he did have a crush on me, who knows? I never thought about it. In retrospect, Hart was probably the first person who saw that I was in love with my friend Rebecca. But he never pushed me to talk about it. He never pushed me to do anything.

Hart was exactly the kind of guy most mothers didn't want on a daughter's arm. He had tattoos and piercings – a barbell through his nose, another in his eyebrow. I never once saw him wear a coat, even in the dead of winter. Mid-February, he'd be wearing long, baggy shorts and a band T-shirt, trudging through the snow in Doc Martens. He looked like a punk, but he was easily the smartest kid in school. You had to talk to him to know that.

When Hart headed to one of those somewhere-out-there universities after high school, I stayed in the city. For whatever reason, an entire year went by where we just weren't in contact. I had so much going on that I didn't really remember he was gone until he called me up one night asking if I wanted to grab a bite.

The moment I walked into the loungy restaurant, Hart

called out my unfortunate if inevitable nickname. 'Anal!'

He picked me up and spun me around and didn't set me down until we were at our table. Everything came streaming back at once: the endless discussions about sex and life and politics and destiny. A year had gone by, and we were right back where we left off.

'I have a girlfriend,' he said, beaming with pride. 'I wanted to tell you in person.'

He pulled a set of prints from the pocket of his cargo shorts and showed me pictures of Sophie in corsets, in garters, in seamed stockings.

I flipped through the pictures, ogling his vixen. 'Damn, Hart, I'm jealous!'

'Sorry, but you had your chance.'

I laughed without meaning to. 'Jealous of *you*, not *her*.' That sounded way more bitchy than I meant it, so I tried to lighten the mood. 'Can I keep this one of your girlfriend in a body stocking?'

'As if!' Hart yanked the pictures out of my hand.

Just as he tucked those snapshots into his pocket, a voice from behind me said, 'I'm wearing that now.'

I whipped my head around, but she was already scooting in beside Hart. The girl in the pictures... This was her, no question. A queasy heat rolled through my belly, painting my face scarlet – I could see it in the mirrored tiles beside our booth.

'Jesus, I'm sorry.' What else could I say after flashing her nearly nude image around the restaurant? 'You're Sophie? Well, obviously you are. I'm Analee.'

'But you can call her Anal,' Hart said as our garlic cheese bread arrived.

'I'm guessing there's a story there,' Sophie cackled.

The pretty boy waiter gave me a look, but I was more interested in the pretty *girl* across the booth.

142

'In high school, the attendance form never had enough spaces for long names.' I was too hungry not to grab some bread, but that didn't stop me from talking. 'Mine was always cut off. On the first day of every semester, if the teacher didn't know me, they'd call out "Valparadiso, Anal ...?"'

'Because the form was last name first, first name last,' Hart said. 'And the two e's at the end of "Analee" were cut off.'

'Thanks, Doctor Redundo. I did put that together.' Sophie's husky voice was steeped in sarcasm, and it made me throb. This girl had it all: curves to die for, a snarky sense of humour, and *God* that lingerie!

'So, your nickname,' Sophie went on. 'Was that a self-fulfilling prophecy? Are you big-time into anal?'

My throat suddenly felt like it was full of cotton. I swallowed hard. Did Hart not tell her I was a lesbian? Nobody read me that way. Plus, I wasn't used to talking about personal stuff with strangers, even if they were knee-buckling beauties.

I stammered, 'I've never actually ... uhh ... tried that.'

'Don't tell me you're still a virgin!' Hart cackled.

'I'm not a virgin. There was a girl ...' I knew my cheeks were glowing, but I didn't want to get into that whole history. 'Well, I've never been with a guy, if that's what you mean. Doubt I ever will, but that's not my barometer for virginity.'

Sophie's expression changed. Suddenly she nodded like she had me all figured out. 'Hart said you had a crush on your best friend but, hell, you've got a full-blown case of the gays!'

'Uhh ... *What?*'

'I'm kidding!' She smacked the table and laughed. 'I'm queer too, can't you tell?'

I didn't know how to answer. Luckily, Hart saved me from silence by saying, 'Sophie's an anal freakazoid.'

'Hells yeah.' Sophie nodded resolutely. 'Feels dirty as fuck. It's bad-girl sex. I love it.'

I stared mutely across the booth.

'Hart's too macho to let me shove anything up his ass.' Sophie laughed when he rolled his eyes. 'Dude doesn't know what he's missing.'

With a shrug, Hart grabbed his second slice of garlic bread. 'Sorry if I'm self-conscious about my anus.'

'What about you, Analee?' Sophie started taking off her silver rings one by one and setting them on the table beside Hart. 'You ever been served from behind?'

'Me?' I felt like a kid, the way they looked at me, anticipating. 'No.'

Sophie shook out her naked fingers. 'Wanna give it a go?'

'What, right here?' This was starting to feel like one of those nightmares where you're forced to go to the bathroom in front of your entire anthropology class.

'Not at the table.' Sophie cackled. 'Jesus, have a little respect for the other patrons! We'll do it in the bathroom.'

I couldn't breathe. 'Do *what*?'

Sophie had already risen from the booth when she said, 'If you don't know, I'm not explaining it.'

I looked to Hart. 'Am I on *Candid Camera*?'

'No,' he said. 'But that doesn't mean you can't smile.'

I sat for a moment, feeling utterly like a deer in the headlights. Hart might have been saying something. Sophie might have been too, but all I could think about were her fingers – the sight of her sliding off those silver rings, and placing them on the table. And Hart didn't mind a bit.

In a daze, I followed Sophie down the back corridor.

The washroom was almost nicer than the restaurant. The countertop was solid and black rock, maybe granite, with little silver flecks throughout. Beside the sink there was a basket of toiletries. Sophie grabbed a tube like she knew just what she was after.

'What's that?' I asked, following her to the second stall. There were only two in total.

'Take a look.' She tossed the little tube over her shoulder and I scrambled to catch it.

'Unscented hypo-allergenic hand lotion?'

'Works in a pinch.' Sophie grabbed me by the wrist and yanked me into the stall.

Before I could wrap my brain around the fact this was really happening, her lips were on mine. Her hot tongue thrashed in my mouth, thick and throbbing. She tasted like garlic, but not in a bad way. Actually, the taste made me hungry for more than just food. I know that sounds corny, but it's true.

When Sophie slammed me against the side of the stall, I clenched my fist around the lotion. Her big breasts crashed against mine. That's when I remembered the first thing she'd said as she came to the table – that she had on that body stocking from the photograph.

I opened my eyes and gasped, struggling to see beyond Sophie's jet-black hair. 'Wait! Why's the door of the stall open?'

Sophie's cat-eyes burned dark. 'Why shouldn't it be?'

'We're gonna get caught!' I felt like a nerd, getting so upset, but this was feeling more and more like my humiliating toilet dream. 'What if someone comes in?'

'I'll close this door if the other one opens.' Sophie held me roughly against the solid stall divider – it was black with silver specks, just like the countertop, and it went all the way down to the floor. 'You scared, Analee?'

My breath felt jagged, spinning from my lungs. Of course I was scared!

'Stay put,' Sophie said. She let go of my shoulders and pulled her black jersey dress over her head.

'You weren't joking,' I stammered.

Underneath, she had on the fishnet body stocking from Hart's photo. No bra. Her dark nipples puckered in the cool air. No panties either. The crotchless lingerie showed off her baby-smooth pussy lips.

'You like?' she asked.

I nodded, astounded. 'It's almost like you planned this.'

Sophie cupped my mound, and an electric sizzle travelled up my body, centralising as a ball of fire way down in my belly. 'Are you wet?'

I laughed wryly, keeping one eye on the open stall door. 'What do you think?'

If another woman walked into the washroom, it's not like she'd automatically see us. Our stall was a good six paces from the door. Maybe that's why, when Sophie threw down my skirt, I stepped out of it, shameless. She tore down my panties. I stepped out of those too, unbuttoned my purple satin blouse, and tossed it on the floor.

'Here, gimme your pussy.' She glided her fingers across my slit, and my knees turned to jelly.

'It's all yours.'

Grabbing my one free hand, she forced it between her legs. 'Mine's wetter.'

My fingers forged a path between her crotchless fishnets. She *was* wetter than me. Her slit drew me in, and I penetrated it with two fingers, then three. Pussy juice dripped down my palm as I went at her, confident and forceful. I had a feeling she thought I didn't know what I

146

was doing, and I wanted to prove her wrong.

'Gimme.' She grabbed the lotion and slathered her middle finger with the stuff.

Pressing me against the slick wall, Sophie asked, 'You ready for this, *Anal*-Lee?'

'Yeah, OK.' Everything seemed to happening in the wrong order, like this bathroom was an alternate reality. I kept glancing out the stall door, fully expecting a circus clown to go by on a unicycle – anything that would indicate this wasn't real life. 'Go for it.'

'Fuck your ass?' Her eyes blazed somewhere between tiger and snake. 'Sure you can handle it?'

The waiting made my insides itch. I still had three fingers inside her pussy, but I pulled them out fast and asked, 'Can *you*?'

She was so close now I couldn't see the look on her face. Her hand went down on me, and I spread my legs for her. I didn't expect her thumb to hook itself into my pussy while her middle finger overshot my slit. Even though I knew to expect an errant digit in my ass, the sensation was sort of shocking when she pressed the pad of her finger against my hole.

When I gasped, she laughed like she couldn't get over how cute I was.

'The skin there is sensitive,' I explained. I hoped she would kiss me again so I wouldn't have to talk.

'How about this?' she growled as her finger pressed through the tight ring of my ass. I couldn't believe how easy it went in. The lotion felt cool around my asshole, but it didn't feel weird or anything.

'That's good.' I clenched my cheeks, trapping the bulk of her hand between them. 'Do you want me to …?'

'Rub your clit.' Her voice was gritty, deep and dark. I started stroking at the apex of her mound, and she hissed, then said, 'No, *your* clit.'

'Mine?' I kept glancing out the door, like her dirty words would summon the public sex police. Her finger and thumb were moving inside me now, pulsing more than thrusting. I thought my heart might leap out my mouth. 'You don't want me to …?'

'I already know how it feels, Anal-Lee.' She backed off a touch and bent from the hips. My gaze went straight to her huge breasts inside that kick-ass body stocking. 'Take off your bra real quick, then work that little clit.'

The moment I'd stripped bare, she dove at my tits and went wild, flicking her tongue back and forth between them. Fleetingly, I wondered what Hart would think if he could see this public display. Maybe later, Sophie would tell him about it as she fucked him. My stomach tumbled at the idea of Hart picturing me with his girlfriend's mouth on my nipple and fingers filling my orifices.

'Ready for another?' she asked, gently withdrawing her finger from my butt.

Once it was out, I wasn't sure if I could even handle that one back inside me, but when would I get another chance? 'Yeah, do it.'

She fucked me with her thumb, pumping so hard I gasped. 'You want it, you gotta play with yourself.'

'Oh God!'

She pounded me and my knees buckled. I couldn't believe that was just her thumb in my cunt.

'Come on, Anal-lover.' Her fist whacked the base of my slit so hard I knew I'd have bruises there tomorrow. 'I want to watch you masturbate.'

That word, *masturbate*, was too dirty, too real. I glanced out the open door, certain some member of my immediate family would be hovering Godzilla-like over the scene. But no. It was just us, Sophie stretching my ass

148

with two fingers and rubbing them against the thumb in my pussy.

She looked up to say, 'Play with your goddamn clit!' and then her mouth was on my tits, teasing them to stiff peaks. Every lick, suck, and nibble made me a little bolder than before. I traced my hand through my pubic hair. My fingers were still wet with her pussy juice when I touched my clit. The lightning-sharp sensation tore through me, straightening my spine, urging my hips to rock against Sophie's hand.

Sophie's hand rocked too, back and forth, a come-hither motion deep in my ass. I'd never felt anything like it before. Her thumb in my pussy was new enough a pleasure, but those fingers in my ass might have put me over the edge even if I hadn't teased my swollen clit.

'Oh God, I'm gonna come.' My voice was gravel, just like Sophie's. Shame had flown out the window, or out the stall door, and now I just wanted to get off. 'I'm gonna come so fucking hard!'

I scoured my clit, feeling the strain in my chest as Sophie opened my ass with a third finger. Maybe that would have been too much at any other time, but I was so close to coming my body was open to any and all pleasures. I writhed against the wall, bucking into her expert hand while I stroked myself off.

The fireworks started in my pelvis, firing down my thighs and up my chest simultaneously. Sophie was still sucking my tits, and that didn't hurt matters. I bit my bottom lip so hard I tasted blood, and still I couldn't hold in the cries. My feet arched until I was up on my tiptoes, banging my shoulders against the stall. My back was sure to be bruised too – add that to the list – but I couldn't contain the orgasmic energy coursing through my body. It took hold of me, driving me into a frenzy of motion. My whole hand scoured my poor clit, slapping Sophie's as she sent me over the edge again and again.

My ass clamped down on her brutal fingers, and I couldn't believe how that beautiful strain kicked up every other pleasure. I knew right away that anal would be my new go-to. I could foresee a day when I wouldn't be able to get off without it.

Squeeeeeeaaaaak!

The bathroom door.

I froze against the wall, feeling caught already, but Sophie didn't break a sweat. She closed the stall door slowly, gently, and smiled as she picked up our clothes. I let the wall hold me up until Sophie kissed me in the perfect near-silence.

After the other woman had left the bathroom, we snuck from our stall and washed our hands. My face was bright red and I had that freshly fucked glow about me, but I looked pretty presentable.

'I feel so naked without my rings,' Sophie said once she'd dried her hands.

The pretty boy waiter shot us a snooty glance as we returned to our booth. Dinner was already on the table, and Hart had started without us, which seemed fair enough.

'So, how did Anal like anal?' He mopped spaghetti sauce from his beard. 'Did Sophie go easy on you?'

'I don't think so,' I replied.

At the same time, she said, 'Yeah, I was gentle.'

As I dug into my lasagne, I couldn't help wondering what a non-gentle ass-fucking from Sophie would feel like. 'Hart, your girlfriend's a super-freak. She wouldn't even close the stall door.'

His eyebrows shot halfway up his forehead as he turned to watch Sophie putting her silver rings back on, finger by finger. When their eyes met, they didn't say anything. They just exchanged this incredibly knowing gaze, smiling that special smile only true loves shared.

I'd told Hart I was jealous when I first saw those pictures of Sophie. Now I'd seen her in the flesh. I'd touched her and kissed her and felt her inside me. She'd pushed my boundaries and stretched me open. What I saw between Sophie and my sweet friend Hart was a relationship that incorporated people like me, and grew stronger for the sharing.

I couldn't be jealous of their love, because their love was mine too.

Strictly Au Naturale
by Anna Sansom

Jessica scanned the appointment list for her next client: *Karen Adams, 45 mins, bikini + leg*. She groaned out loud and glanced up at the large clock on the wall behind the reception desk. She had just five minutes to compose herself and prepare the room for Karen. There would be 45 minutes of pain and then it would all be over for another four weeks. Of course the pain would all be Jessica's: Karen Adams was one of the most annoying, obnoxious, and difficult women Jessica had ever met. She slammed the appointment book closed and rushed upstairs to check the wax was up to temperature and everything was in place. Then she adopted a pretend smile and steeled herself for Karen's arrival.

The worst bit about Karen Adams was her complete lack of respect for her own or anyone else's dignity. 'Hubby's whisking me off to Barbados!' she announced as soon as she was through the door. 'I want my vag clean as a whistle.' Then she popped a couple of ibuprofen, kicked off her shoes, and pulled her skirt and knickers down. She left her clothes in a pile at the side of the treatment table and climbed on top. 'Right, let's get it over with,' she said and opened her legs wide.

Jessica grabbed a towel and draped it over Karen's middle before bending down to pick up the discarded

153

clothes and shoes and move them to the chair at the side of the room. 'So you want the full Monty this time?' she asked.

'Yep, you're going to have to check my butthole too. I promised him I'd be like a virgin bride for our holiday.' Karen giggled. 'I've been doing my Kegels like nobody's business – I could hold a pencil up there for a good half an hour now! Nice and tight, that's what he's getting.'

Jessica shuddered inwardly. Karen always gave too much information, and the images her words conjured in Jessica's imagination of a randy Mr Adams and his pube-free "virgin bride" were not at all pleasant. She tested the wax temperature on the inside of her wrist and took a deep breath. 'OK then, I'll just take the towel away now.'

Jessica gratefully slipped out of her uniform and into her street clothes once the last client had left the building. She usually took her make-up off before leaving but tonight she was in a hurry to get home. She transformed herself daily from "real Jessica" into "beautician Jessica" with the aid of the salon's tester pots and her white tunic and trouser two-piece. It was a matter of principle to Jessica that how she portrayed herself at work was completely different to how she looked out of work. She did as much as she needed to in order to meet the salon's strict image policies and was grateful that there was no requirement to have long nails in addition to the necessity for make-up.

The make-up could stay on for the duration of the bus ride home if it meant that Jessica could be back in time for the final episode of the psychological thriller she'd been watching on TV. If the bus was prompt, she would have just enough time to stick a lasagne in the microwave, pour herself a large glass of pinot, and settle down to find out who the killer was and what the motive had been all along.

The bus was late. Jessica tapped her foot impatiently. A couple of older women to her left were complaining about the wait and glaring at the younger ones taking up all the space on the bench. The younger ones were oblivious: each had their head down and was tapping and swiping at the small screen of their phone. Jessica picked her phone out of her bag and typed in her pass number. No calls, no messages. No surprise there. She dropped it back into her bag and willed the bus to arrive.

'This is ridiculous,' Jessica muttered after another 15 minutes had passed and there was still no sign of her bus.

'I hope there hasn't been an accident,' a voice replied from her right.

Jessica turned to see who had spoken. The woman had short, tousled hair and was wearing baggy jeans and a hooded sweatshirt at least three sizes too big for her. 'Last time it was late,' the woman went on, 'there had been a collision on the high street. The bus couldn't get past for ages. Someone had been knocked down on the crossing – a boy, I think – by a guy on a motorbike. Apparently the police made the bus driver wait till they'd got statements and witnesses and all that.'

'I hope that's not what's happened this time,' Jessica said, feeling a bit guilty in case anything like that *had* happened and here she was getting cross about missing the start of a TV programme.

'Are you going to Harrington?' the woman asked. ''Cos you can walk to Petershill Road and pick up the number 16. I'm going to do that. Had enough of waiting.'

'I may as well,' Jessica said with one last, longing glance up the street.

'I'm Trudi,' the woman introduced herself as they turned away from the bus stop.

'Jessica.'

They walked in an uncomfortable silence. Jessica had spent all day making polite conversation and really didn't want to have to continue all the way to Petershill Road.

'Just finished work?' Trudi broke the silence.

'Yep.'

'What do you do?'

'I work at a beauty salon.' Jessica hated admitting this to someone who obviously didn't care much about their appearance.

'Cool. You must get used to seeing women in the buff. All those seaweed wraps and Brazilians. I've always thought it must be weird to strip off in front of a total stranger and let them do stuff to you. But I suppose it's quite normal for you.'

'You get used to it.' Jessica had a vision of Karen Adams brazenly opening her legs and pulling her thighs close to her chest so she could check for any missed hairs.

'So you do that? The Brazilians and stuff?' Trudi laughed. 'Looking at fannies all day – what a job.'

They walked on in silence. Jessica knew that social convention dictated she should now politely ask about Trudi's job but she couldn't be bothered. She'd never see this woman again once they got to Petershill Road so what did matter *what* Trudi did to earn money?

'You'd probably get a fright if you saw mine,' Trudi confided. 'I'm strictly au naturale. I favour the full minge. Nice and bushy.'

'Not everyone goes for the Brazilian: some just want a trim and a tidy, you know, just the bits that show,' Jessica told her. She felt the need to justify her work somehow. After all, the women came to her; she never forced anyone to have a bikini wax. 'Most women, well, *a lot* of women, prefer to be tidy.'

'What about you?'

Jessica felt herself blush; no one had ever enquired about her own pubic preferences before. 'Just the edges,' she admitted, picking up her walking pace to try and get to the next bus stop so she could get home and finally get some time to herself.

'I would have guessed that,' Trudi told her. 'You look like a woman who likes to be tidy. Here we are: Petershill Road. Oh, and there's a bus just turned the corner. Brilliant.' Trudi stuck her arm out to signal to the driver to stop. 'After you,' she said to Jessica. 'I'm going to carry on walking; I'm not far from home now anyway. See ya.'

Jessica gave a small wave to Trudi from her seat on the bus but Trudi didn't look up. She leant back against the seat and checked her watch: her TV plans had been ruined.

The next day Jessica had just put the finishing touches to her make-up when the receptionist appeared in the staff changing room. 'Jessica, I've got a new client outside who asked for waxing appointment with you. I would have booked her in but she looks a bit – well, *odd*. I thought you might want to sneak a peek at her before you accept the booking.'

Curious, she followed the receptionist to the glass door leading into the waiting area and peered into the room. Although she had her back to the door, Jessica recognised the woman's outline immediately: baggy clothes and a short, shaggy haircut, it had to be Trudi.

'It's all right,' Jessica said, 'I'll take her.' She walked into the room and approached Trudi. 'Hello again.'

'Hello!' Trudi smiled broadly as she turned around. 'Thought I'd give your waxing a go. Upstairs, is it? You lead the way.'

'So you decided it was time for a change?' Jessica asked as she steered Trudi down the corridor and into her room. 'I thought you were a fan of "au naturale".' She wheeled the cart with the waxing equipment towards the treatment table. 'Just slip off your jeans. Keep your undies on for now until we've decided how much you want off.'

Trudi unbuckled her belt and stepped out of her jeans. She perched on the edge of the table, still wearing her shoes and socks.

Jessica looked up from the wax pot. 'Oh, you're wearing boxers.'

'Is that a problem?'

'Well, normally women come in wearing their bikini briefs. You know, so I can see how much – er – *overgrowth* there is. I'll give you some paper pants to put on instead.' She handed Trudi a small, rolled-up pair of pants. 'Thong bit goes at the back,' she prompted. 'I'll just turn around for a minute.'

When she turned back around, Trudi was lying on the table and wearing the paper pants. Her boxers were draped on the chair along with her jeans.

'Right then. If it's your first time I usually recommend just a tidy to begin with. It can take a while to get used to the sensation.'

'Do you ever get embarrassed? You know, what with it being so intimate and everything,' Trudi placed her hands behind her head and smiled up at Jessica.

'No, it's my job. Are *you* feeling embarrassed or uncomfortable?'

'Not at all; I'm looking forward to it.'

Jessica pretended to check the temperature of the wax pot. *She* was feeling uncomfortable with the situation. For a newbie, Trudi seemed way too relaxed and at ease. Then there were those boxer shorts: they weren't fashionable *girl shorts*, they were proper men's ones. She doubted there had ever been a pair of men's boxers in the salon before. Not that she had any problem with Trudi wearing them: if anything they looked kind of cute on her and they matched the cheeky, boyish style that Trudi carried off so well. In fact, the more she thought about it, if this had been any setting other than the salon, Jessica would be enjoying this exchange with the other woman. Preparing to wax her felt quite sexual and unfamiliar, even though it was a procedure she'd done hundreds of times before.

Jessica leant over Trudi and gestured with a wooden spatula. 'I can take away these hairs here –' she drew an imaginary line in the air above the side of the temporary briefs '– and here –' She indicated the other side. 'You can keep those on and we'll use them as a template.'

'I was hoping to take them off.'

'You want me to wax off more?'

'No, I just want to take my pants off for you.' Trudi propped herself up on an elbow as Jessica took a step back from the table. 'To be honest, I don't want you to wax *anything*. But I would like you to come on a date with me.'

Jessica laughed with surprise and relief. 'All this just to ask me out?'

'Well, I tried last night, but you were obviously not in the mood to notice someone flirting with you,' Trudi told her matter-of-factly.

'You have some strange ideas about flirting.' Jessica pointed to the paper pants and both women laughed.

'I tell you what: either come out with me tonight *or* you're going to have to give me a Brazilian. Which is it to be?' Trudi replaced her hands behind her head and grinned wickedly.

Jessica glanced at the clock. 'Your time's nearly up; I guess I'll have to take you up on the date.'

'Great!' Trudi swung herself off the table. 'Now turn around so I can get dressed. I'm not giving you any more advance previews.'

The day passed quickly and Jessica made sure to finish her last appointment on time. The bus arrived on schedule and Jessica was ready for her date in record time. It had been several months since she'd last had a date and excitement overtook any nerves she was feeling. She liked Trudi and she was amused by the method the woman had used to ask her out. If nothing else, it should be a fun evening. Anything more than a few laughs and a nice meal would be a bonus.

'Woah, you look different!' Trudi appraised Jessica without make-up. 'Even lovelier than before,' she added.

'You look different too.' Jessica took in the fitted jeans and vest top under Trudi's leather jacket and smiled her approval. There was an awkward moment of silence as they looked at each other, then Trudi pulled open the restaurant door and held it open for Jessica to enter. Cute, Jessica thought, and walked into the bustling hubbub of a Friday night eatery.

She was right about an evening of laughter and good food. The meal and the company were great and Jessica found herself warming more and more to Trudi. Jessica giggled as Trudi flirted easily and charmingly with the waitress and got them a free desert. They ate it with one spoon and both openly watched each other's lips and tongues feeding on the smooth and creamy panna cotta.

Next Trudi ordered them coffee and brandy and they moved from the dining area to a more dimly lit sofa in the bar. Trudi sat close beside Jessica and casually placed her hand on Jessica's thigh. 'Were you tempted earlier?' she asked.

'Tempted by what?' Jessica leant her thigh closer to Trudi's.

'To get me out of those paper pants.' Trudi smiled mischievously.

'No. I'm always totally professional in the salon,' Jessica said, poker-faced. Then, unable to stop herself smiling, she added, 'I'm very tempted now, though.'

'That's a shame.' Now it was Trudi's turn to deadpan.

'Oh. Why?' Jessica drew her thigh away a little from Trudi's touch.

'Because unless you have a stash of paper pants at your house we're going to have to make do with removing the real thing back at mine.' Trudi held her gaze as Jessica processed the implications of her last statement.

They tumbled through Trudi's front door and she led the way straight to the bedroom. The room was pretty messy and Jessica stood for a moment, taking in the scene. There were piles of books by the bed, CDs scattered on the floor beside the stereo, and the bedclothes lay in a rumpled heap. The room was lit by an angle-poise lamp directed onto the bed. Trudi ignored her scattered possessions and tilted the lamp to point at the ceiling. 'There,' she said, 'how's that for an ambience?'

Jessica laughed. The setting was so different to their earlier encounter in the salon: there, having women bare their pussies to her was all part of the job; here she could hardly wait for Trudi to strip off and show her more of what she'd glimpsed on her salon table.

'Last night, when we were walking to the bus stop,' Jessica began, 'you said you thought it was weird to strip off in front of a stranger and have them do stuff to you. I'm guessing you don't mind doing it now?'

Now it was Trudi's turn to laugh. 'We've just had dinner together; that means we're not strangers. But to answer your original question: no, I have no qualms whatsoever about getting naked with you and letting you have your way with me. Just as long as there's no wax involved.'

'No wax,' Jessica reassured as she unbuttoned Trudi's jeans.

'I should warn you I lied earlier; I'm not wearing any underwear.'

'Even better.' Jessica slipped her hand inside Trudi's jeans and cupped her mound, feeling the springy hairs underneath her palm. Trudi pushed her jeans down around her knees and then slid Jessica's fingers further down, through her hairs, until she made contact with Trudi's slick lips and the nub of her clit. Jessica pressed her fingers against Trudi and felt the urgent throb of her own desire. She manoeuvred Trudi to the edge of the bed. 'Lie down and spread 'em,' she joked. She let go of Trudi and quickly removed her own clothes. Trudi followed suit, then pulled Jessica down onto the bed with her. Rolling on top, Trudi pressed her body onto Jessica's. They began to kiss: gentle, explorative kisses that quickly became more confident and demanding. Jessica reached her arms around Trudi and pulled her closer to her, feeling their breasts squash together and their hips join in a rhythmic dance. Needing even more contact, Trudi shifted her weight to one side and positioned her thigh between Jessica's legs. Jessica gratefully squeezed around her, feeling her own slickness coating Trudi's thigh.

Trudi's kisses left Jessica's mouth and began to travel a path down her body. She kissed her throat and her collarbone, then the space between Jessica's breasts, then she boldly sucked one of Jessica's nipples into her mouth. She rolled the other nipple between her thumb and finger, feeling both react to her touch with their puckering and hardening, and Jessica react to the strong sensations by squirming beneath her.

Next Trudi kissed Jessica's stomach, working a slow path closer and closer to Jessica's pubes. Trudi brushed them with her fingertips and Jessica raised her hips instinctively, trying to bring her cunt into contact. Trudi kissed Jessica's mound, teasing the exposed skin that had been cleared of hair. It felt soft and silky and Trudi nuzzled into it, brushing first with her lips and then with the lightest flick of her tongue. Jessica groaned. Trudi's tongue travelled further to lick and taste the inside of Jessica's thighs and she inhaled deeply to breathe in the glorious scent of Jessica's arousal.

With Jessica's pubic hair trimmed and tidied, Trudi had a clear view of the shape of her cunt: long, butterfly lips curving up to a shining clit standing proudly outside of its hood. She ran her tongue between Jessica's lips and up and over her clit. Jessica groaned again and took hold of Trudi's hair. Trudi repeated her action but this time dipped inside Jessica with the tip of her tongue. Feeling the pressure of Jessica's hands on the back of her head, Trudi pushed her tongue in deeper.

'Lick me,' Jessica gasped and Trudi brought her tongue back to Jessica's clit. She stroked and circled over and around Jessica's hard nub, matching the speed and rhythm of Jessica's hips as they danced on the bed.

When Jessica's body suddenly quietened, Trudi quickened her pace, carefully staying on the one spot that held Jessica's full focus. She felt her swell and harden even more before time seemed to pause for a moment and

Jessica cried out. They tipped over the edge together and time picked them up, now travelling super-fast as Jessica's hips bucked and shook, milking every last sensation from Trudi's face pressed firmly against her.

A smiling Trudi raised her flushed and drenched face from Jessica's lap and she wriggled up the bed to kiss her mouth once more. Jessica tasted her juices on Trudi's lips and felt a small aftershock of lust jolt through her loins. 'You're amazing,' she whispered, her eyes wide and her cheeks rosy.

'So are you,' Trudi replied, gazing adoringly at the gorgeous woman on her bed.

Jessica snaked an arm down between their bodies and felt again the springy hairs of Trudi's untamed bush. The ends of the hairs were curled into tight locks and were wet with Trudi's need. Jessica's fingers found an easy path through the forest and moved smoothly inside Trudi's waiting cunt. She rocked her hand against Trudi and allowed her fingers to be drawn in deeper.

Their faces were so close that they could each feel the other's breath warm on their skin. Trudi moved even closer and kissed Jessica slowly while moving her arm down between their bodies to make contact with her own clit. Jessica felt the tips of Trudi's fingertips brush the heel of her hand and pressed her tongue more urgently into Trudi's mouth. She broke away from the kiss just long enough to murmur, 'You touching yourself is so hot.'

Jessica matched the pace of her tongue in Trudi's mouth to the pace of her fingers in her enrobed pussy. Trudi stroked herself in synchrony, so deeply held in Jessica's hypnotic spell that she was unable to change tempo or direction. Jessica was the conductor and Trudi her accompanist, and the symphony was reaching its climax.

The spell was broken when the intensity of the sensations in Trudi's body exceeded her ability to remain focused on Jessica's actions. She pulled away from the kiss and called out, 'I'm gonna come!' She clamped around Jessica's hand, stilling any further movements in her cunt, and her fingers circled her clit in a frenzied action. Her back arched off the bed, her legs went rigid, and then her whole body shook as her orgasm sped through her body.

Later, as they lay side by side, Jessica trailed her fingers dreamingly through Trudi's pubes, while Trudi stroked patterns over Jessica's thighs. 'I'm thinking of coming into the salon again tomorrow,' Trudi said, 'to get a bit of a trim and tidy.'

'Leave them alone; I like them just the way they are,' Jessica told her, patting the hairs into place. 'But how about you come into the salon anyway? There are plenty of other things I can do with your wonderful pussy instead.'

Wake Up Call
by Elise Hepner

I hunkered down beneath the cheap, glue-scented wooden desk a little before daybreak, knowing Melina would be seated in front of the cameras before her morning shift. She always liked to practice several times before going live on the air – as if it were her first time every time. The nerves were cute, but I was becoming sick of the way she wound herself up. Sometimes I was sure the make-up artists didn't want to apply another layer of caked-on expensive product because she'd been puking in the bathroom again. So if it took a little experimentation to get her used to the camera, I was willing to do whatever it took to keep my show successful. Including playing this rousing game of hide and seek.

My knees ached and my mouth was dry. But that'd be fixed soon enough. A quick consultation with my watch and the click-clacking of high heels on concrete was a sure sign that Melina was here. No one else came in so early except for me. The cadence grew quicker. With it the beat of my pulse in my fingers pounded as I laced them together around my bent legs. When the chair pulled backward, I nearly gasped with the taste of her orchid perfume – always a little too much – on my tongue. She cleared her throat, took a seat, and I restrained myself from stroking her soft leg through her stockings, knowing that she'd be freshly shaved and beyond beautiful beneath my fingertips. Not time yet. As she pulled herself into place I fought against the back of the desk. An angling game for space that she didn't know I was there yet. The timing had to be perfect.

With my hand trembling like a schoolgirl's at her first dance, I took my cell phone out of my pocket and pressed "send". One delightful ping from above. And Melina's small noise of shock, masked as if someone in the studio could hear her despite all the lights being out and no one milling around yet. Her low, descending laugh speckled goosebumps across my bare skin. And I waited to see if she'd comply with my demands while tucking my phone back in my pocket and giving into the small smile that had been trying to climb my face all day. She scooted back from the desk. I could almost see the goofy grin and soft blush climbing her face as she stood and probably shot a cautious glance in both directions. Seconds later I had the privilege of watching her kick off her expensive shoes, strip off her stockings, and throw both into a heap under the circular desk.

But the best was yet to come.

Melina crouched down and wiggled a bit. Only reason I could tell was from the cute pointed toes look she sported since my viewpoint was mid-thigh downward – but it was a sweet view. As her red panties slipped down to her ankles I bit back a moan and folded myself tighter into the shadows. When she kicked them under the table and slipped her heels back on, I couldn't resist snatching them up from the broadcasting floor, bringing her sweet scent to my nose. I planned on being covered in that scent in a matter of minutes. Until I worked all day with the memory of my lover warm on my tongue. Despite the fact that I couldn't wait to get started with my plan, I waited until she sat down on the rolling chair and pulled herself back into the table. A shuffling of papers. She would be preparing her note cards for the morning broadcast.

Without the small spotlight that lit her up, I could only make out the bare outline of her legs as she pressed them together. Did she think of me as her thighs flexed? I turned my head to keep my breath from her bare skin. I couldn't bear to startle her quite yet. Just another moment listening to her recite her lines. Sometimes when we were in bed all I wanted for her to do was read to me. I'd dragged cereal boxes into bed so she would chime off the nutritional values table in her sweet, soft voice that somehow wound up so damn commanding I'd stop everything to follow her lead. As I skimmed my fingertips along my jaw line, I thought of her sweet touch. My tongue passed over my lips.

'Lights, camera, action,' I whispered, digging my phone out of my pocket again and sending my last text message as soon as I heard the doors to the studio opening. Other people would be here soon. Prime time. Took me at least two minutes to type out the message because my hands were shaking so badly as my pulse roared against my temples in the sweetest adrenaline rush.

Don't freak out.

Three little words that, if they weren't heeded, were going to define a lot of actions in the next few seconds. Barely breathing, I gently skimmed my fingers up her ankle – and though she jerked back, she didn't scream. We were doing good. When she uncrossed her legs it was a nice little sign of acceptance. A jolt of sharp satisfaction made my cramped surroundings almost livable for the barest hint of a second. I continued my journey with my fingers, steadily rising higher from the knee to press a lingering palm across her inner thighs. I watched her toes flex in her open-toed heels and chuckled to myself. With the smallest touch I could imagine the subtle, peachy flush working up her cheeks. She was in the palm of my hand, both literally and figuratively, as her muscles tensed beneath her soft, newly moisturised skin.

One minute more to appreciate the delicate touch while her voice quavered on a word that went in one ear and out the other. My ears were perked to the sounds of the studio. Voices. Doors opening and closing. A tech being berated for being late with the doughnuts yesterday. The room was slowly filling up, and I had my girl tied to her chair with my touch. There was no way she was leaving, not when someone could discover me beneath the desk, and wouldn't that be a juicy little rumour to spread around on set? Not like we were a secret – though we were very much so. While her whole world filled up with people coming to do their jobs, mine filled with the scent of her arousal as I pried her legs apart further, and drew closer until my hot breath was a tease across her naked pussy lips.

When she grabbed the edge of the desk all I could see was the moulted white of her thumbs. Another deliberate, testing blow across her clit, and her foot shot forward, almost kicking me. Easy, tiger. My hand squeezed her inner thigh, reminding her not to do damage or show anyone what was really going on down here, while my other started to move sweet, simple circles against her hard, wet clit. Footsteps. Her trill voice chirping to the make-up lady as she did a touch-up, I pinched her clit until she laughed because she couldn't moan. I'm sure that got a look, because nothing the other woman had said was even remotely funny. God, this spin on news made the day so much more lively. I couldn't say I wasn't tempted to do it every morning – but then she'd catch on.

Small strokes and teases while her arousal took over the glue scent from before and I couldn't wait any longer to have her on my mouth. We were going from warm-up to the main event. My mouth watered while I picked up bits and pieces of her conversation before putting my lips against her silky warmth and rubbing my mouth from clit to the bottom of her slit. To her credit, she didn't move a single inch. Not even when I traversed the same slick flesh with my tongue and relished her sweet juices. Every second I put my mouth on her was a moment to remember – but having people so close to us while I did it? With no idea? It gave me new meaning to my idea of relationship spontaneity while I flicked her clit with my tongue and she gently bucked up her hips for more. That's my girl. Now she was starting to catch on quite well, and for that, she should be rewarded.

One hard, long suck on her clit. And all the while mine begged for attention as I focused the entirety of my pussy-licking expertise on my lover, who was currently in a heated discussion with the cameraman. I raked my fingernails down her inner thigh to make sure she was still paying attention to me. And her delightful full body shudder against my mouth was answer enough. Could I get her eyes to roll back in her head in front of 15 million morning show viewers? I tongued her slit to the time of my thundering pulse as her inner walls clenched tight around me. A shiver made goosebumps slip beneath my thigh-highs while air pressed up against my panties with my legs open to get just the right angle inside my lover. She cleared her throat and I flicked her clit with my thumb.

So hot, tight, and perfect against my tongue that my nipples pebbled beneath my bra. A series of flicks against her sensitive nub made sensation shudder up and down

171

her legs as she kicked out and I focused my lips on sucking her clit into my mouth.

'We're on in five, Melina.'

'Sure Charlie, sounds great,' she squeaked out as her perfectly manicured nails drummed against the desk to the tonguing of her clit.

'Too much coffee this morning? Maybe you should cut back. There's nothing to be nervous about today, just a simple ASPCA story and a weather report. You'll be great.'

Melina must have nodded because she was dead silent now that someone had called her out on her betraying finger-tapping. Though it meant I had less to sync my rhythm on as I bit down on her clit. She shifted with a barely audible whimper. But I knew that sound. God, how I wished I could suck on her little pierced nipples. No one on the show except wardrobe knew about that little secret. But she made the sweetest mewling noise while I played with the stainless steel jewellery – as if she'd be perfectly content for me to never move again. More than ever I wanted her to have to hide that noise now, in front of all these good people that she made us hide from – because job loss or no job loss, I wanted them to know my pride in keeping Melina happy. In keeping her at all, really.

She was an incredible woman. And that incredible, indescribable woman deserved to come until she was a mere puddle in her shoes. Which motivated me to slip two fingers inside her, anchoring my grip against her G-spot and pushing in light rhythm to my tongue drawing nonsense against her clit. She took eager breaths in small sips while my large gulps weren't enough. I couldn't get enough of her anywhere on my body. My fingers picked up speed in an in-and-out rhythm that curled her toes while the large spotlights were turned on from above us and the studio hummed with morning life.

She'd be coming soon and it would be my privilege to coax it out on air, live, for the whole world to see – well, to kind of see. I didn't want to get Melina fired. Unable to ignore myself any longer, I shifted my unoccupied hand to cup my pussy against the silky satin of my panties. I rubbed us both off with my lips sealed around her clit and my hands occupied while she mumbled and quaked above me. While I writhed, fighting to stay up on my knees, I wondered if my well-timed thrusts would leave a spot on her suit skirt and I stifled a giggle. But my little giggle soon turned into a lip-biting moan that I couldn't let slide. As much as I loved the idea of making wonderful noises against my lover's pussy, that might be a little loud for the microphone that was attached to her somewhere. And I didn't need the sound guys on to us.

'You ready?'

'Yessss.' Melina fought back a cough, and what I wouldn't give to see her face.

'On in five.'

I moved so quickly against her that her juices smeared across my mouth, coating my fingers. With every sharp breath she filled my lungs while I manipulated my nub with my other thumb. Driven, I fucked her as hard as I could without making the chair roll back by itself.

'Four.'

Ecstatic, my thoughts whirling. Hands preoccupied while an orgasm twisted low in my belly.

'Three.'

My triumph was near – I could literally taste it. My own wetness played across my fingers through my panties and I humped my hand. Melina's inner walls squeezed tighter around my fingers. Little bucks of her hips against my aching mouth.

'Two.'

Did I have enough time? I would make it enough time.

'One.'

While I tumbled into orgasm I shifted my hand away from my cunt and shifted it underneath Melina's skirt until my wet finger was rimming the tight pucker of her anus. Another small, imperceptible wiggle of her ass.

'Good morning, Pottstown –'

Whatever she said from there was a blur against the glaring cacophony inside my head. Lightheaded sparks skipped across my closed eyelids as I closed my lips around Melina's clit. Her heels tip-tapped against the floor as I pulled my fingers almost out of her cunt before ramming them back to the hilt as she coughed through a segment about parking meters. Pleasure twisted low in my gut, wringing my brain of all thoughts. Her inner walls twitched as I fought against her impending orgasm, still reeling from my own. One quick swipe with my other finger along her backdoor and she ground back against the seat, voice squeaking out.

Would anyone be on to our little secret? The idea of the cameramen filming our little tryst while the whole world watched made me pause in my attentive licks to my lover's slit. Let her get a little break before sending her over the edge again. One couldn't get more secretive voyeur than this set-up. Completely perfect, if I said so myself – and I would say it, once we were clear of the sound stage and I could corner Melina in her dressing room for more fun. This was certainly a fantasy I had no plans of abandoning late at night, alone, with my hand, and the heaviness of her cunt in my mind.

Now her delicious juices smeared against my mouth and she went eerily silent above me. I could picture her scrunched-up face, the flush beneath her cheeks, and her

174

lips parted in an "o" of shock. Sure to be an online video favourite once the broadcast clip hit the internet. And all I could say for myself was that I wasn't in the least bit sorry. While Melina's segment wound down and she announced we were going to the weather report for the day, I eased out of her wet cunt, and slid my other hand out from under her ass with a small, possessive squeeze. She was mine, lest she ever forget it. Regardless of the fact that we worked together – in and out of the bedroom – I relished the devilishness of our actions and her helplessness to stop me as I molested her on air.

With my orgasm slowly fading and her sweetness on my tongue, I hunched back under the desk, waiting for the broadcast to end. We only had 359 more to shoot before the end of the year. And they were all opportunities to catch Melina off guard. To play my little games and watch her come face to face with the realisation that she more than enjoyed them. Sounded like the perfect career to me. An immense satisfaction wrapped around me like a warm blanket as I palmed my lover's panties and tucked them into my pocket. Unable to suppress the fine shaking threading through my fingertips I didn't even attempt to text her again with a little self-congratulatory note.

Instead, I allowed my fingers to linger down the line of her leg, which was as close to cuddling as I'd get in the near future. There was a full day of work ahead once the camera crews left for lunch and I was safe to pop out from my hiding spot. Sure, Melina might be a little cross with me. But I didn't have a single regret, knowing that I'd helped us both, and the media attention from her odd broadcast would pitch our small-time news station to PR heights of excellence. I'd done my job twofold. Now hopefully I'd have that explanation available when Melina got a hold of me. A shiver made my whole body writhe at the idea of her in charge, hot with rage, and willing to do anything to pay me back for my little stunt.

I awaited her payback with something close to anticipation, knowing the icing on the cake was Melina having to walk around set all day in a short little skirt with nothing underneath. She'd think of me with every single step. With a silent sigh, I relished my job. Sometimes personal and professional lives needed to collide for the best of both worlds.

And I wouldn't consider myself anything other than lucky.

Hungry Girls
by Angel Propps

'Are you nervous?'

'Why would I be? It's just a blind date, no big deal.'
My words held all the bravado I could muster up but I
could tell by the way that Carrie lifted her right eyebrow
she wasn't fooled at all. Her words made sure I knew she
saw right through me. 'Come off it, Jules, you haven't
been on a date since the break-up. When was that again,
1999?'

'It was six months ago, thank you very much,' I
snapped.

'There's no shame in being nervous.'

'I'm not nervous!'

Then why does your bedroom look like a war zone?'

I looked around the room. Dresses were tossed across
the bed and a dozen pair of shoes had been tumbled into
an untidy heap outside the closet door. A pair of stockings
with a run in one lay crumpled into a ball on the floor. My
dresser was cluttered with cosmetics and brushes and the
smell of perfume rode the air. I sighed and sat down on
the bed, my nerve totally gone.

'I am nervous,' I said. 'I mean, I haven't even wanted
to go out. Hell, I'm not sure I want to tonight even. I
know you said Alex is great, but what if I can't think of
anything to say? What if I bore her senseless or she bores

me or what if I hate her on sight?'

'Worse things have happened,' was her laconic reply. 'Besides, it's a free meal, how can that be a bad thing?'

Since Carrie was a struggling actress who often dated just so she would have dinner I could see why she would think that way, but I was not sold on the idea. I walked into my bathroom and checked my reflection.

I was wearing my favourite red dress, an Audrey Hepburn-inspired number that fit tightly across my small breasts and waist and flared out a bit over the curve of my hip and thighs. The colour went well with my pale skin and blonde hair and the red lipstick I had applied to my full mouth. Sheer stockings with a thin black backseam and lacy red tops, a pair of solid black pumps with three-inch heels and a red Lucite bracelet completed my outfit. I had to admit I looked pretty good but the anxiety stayed anyway.

Carrie was gone when I wandered back into my bedroom. I could hear her rummaging around in the kitchen so I knew she wasn't going out, which meant I couldn't just stay home and say I went out. A flash of inspiration struck and I went to my small nightstand and opened the bottom drawer, rummaged around in it, and pulled out my harness and cock. I pulled it on, making sure that the cock was fitted snugly into its hole. I pulled my dress back down. The poof of the skirt kept the cock hidden. I flipped the skirt up, entranced by the sight of my cock against the red of my skirt. Suddenly I felt better. I tossed the frilly black underwear I had been wearing to the floor, grabbed my purse, and headed for the door, strutting just a bit, the cock bouncing as I stepped down.

'Well, don't you look like somebody who is going out for the sheer hell of it?' Carrie said around a mouthful of cereal and milk. 'Score me some dinner, would you?

178

Bring your roommate a doggie bag. Or order me a meal and make her pay for it if you hate her.'

'Sure thing,' I said and stepped through the door.

Out on the sidewalk I was acutely aware of the cock I sported. I opened my legs a little wider; enjoying the weight and the sensation that I was doing something very, very naughty. The base of it rubbed against my clit in a pleasant way. I could feel my clit swelling and hardening beneath that pressure, and little trickles of fluid soaked into my inner thighs. My nipples tightened, and by the time I had walked the eight blocks to the restaurant I was so aroused my face was flushed and my breathing erratic.

'Jules?'

I was so caught up in the sensations playing out in my body I had not noticed the woman seated on a small bench set behind a few shrubs and flowers. At my name I stared around at her and felt my jaw drop.

She was gorgeous: short, black hair chopped into a deliberately messy cut, large, grey eyes, and a very kissable mouth. Her body was lean and long; she wore a plain white button-down shirt, the top few buttons undone, charcoal-coloured slacks and shoes shined so well they reflected back light. Carrie had said my date was good-looking; she had not told me she exuded a sexual energy so raw my toes tingled just looking at her.

'Alex?' Nerves made my voice a shade too high and I swallowed hard. I took a step forward to take the hand she held out and the cock swung a bit, reminding me of its presence. That courage came back, making my nerves settle. 'It's nice to meet you.'

Her eyes went down, and when they came back up a grin tugged at the corners of her lips. I didn't have to look down; a small breeze had sprung up and the lower half of my dress had flattened against my body for a brief moment. I knew she had seen the outline of my dick, plump and long, jutting out from my body. What was more, I knew she liked it.

She opened the door for me and we stepped into the dim, garlic-scented warmth of the restaurant. Alex asked for a booth and then guided me to it, her long fingers resting gently on the small of my back. The touch sent tingles up my spine.

The booth sat in a dim corner and the leather-covered sides of it rose high and warm around us. A candle glowed in a small, clear holder in the centre of the table, and I caught sight of my prick arching up as I sat down, then the voluminous white tablecloth covered my red-skirted lap. The tiny flame cast light and shadows across the booth that could not disguise the amusement in her eyes.

We ordered dinner and a bottle of rich red wine. The steward brought the bottle and decanted it, poured and left. The quiet grew deeper; it was an hour before the average dinner rush, one of the reasons why I had chosen the time, and we had the place pretty much to ourselves.

'So Carrie says you're a lawyer. Immigration, is that right?'

'Yes. And you're a writer?'

'Mostly I'm a waitress.'

She grinned. 'The waitress at the place I ate breakfast is a dancer. It's this city, I think. Everyone has a dream and they come here to make it come true. It's part of what I love about my job, seeing people reaching for their dream.'

If I hadn't been smitten before I was then. She moved a tiny bit closer to me. Her body heat pressed into my side and I let my body relax so that I was reaching for her without moving. She sensed that subtle shift and her lips

180

opened in a soft smile that revealed small, even teeth.

Her hand brushed my leg, a casual little sweep that lit up my nerve endings. Her wine-scented breath blew across my cheek and my nipples tightened until they were almost painfully erect. The fabric of my dress chafed at them deliciously and her fingers toyed with the hem of my dress.

'Are you ready?' The waiter stood poised by the table, eyes glazed with boredom and his pen poised over the pad he held. I had the juvenile urge to giggle at the irony of the words he had used, but managed to order my meal quietly instead.

Her fingers had left my thigh but the warmth of them remained. We chatted while we waited for our food, idle little talk that passed the time. Alex was amusing and we had a lot of common interests; my fears of being bored had ended as soon as I put on my harness but, sitting there listening to her talk, I almost forgot I was wearing it.

Until our food arrived, that is. Alex spread her napkin across her lap and said, 'Try this.' She forked up a mouthful of tender sea bass in a rich sauce and brought it to my lips. 'Don't chew, just let it lie on your tongue,' she instructed. I did and her other hand went under my skirt, made delicate little passes across the tops of my thighs, playing with lacy edge of my stockings. 'Now,' she said softly into my ear and a shiver shot down my spine as I closed my eyes and chewed and her hand went to my cock.

I could feel the powerful pump she gave my dick; it drew the bottom of my dress up tight against the back and sides of my thighs. The flavour of the food, the scent of her cologne, and the graphic nature of her hand motion all combined in a moment of sheer decadent pleasure.

She didn't stop with one bite, she kept it going. She

put food in my mouth and her other hand stroked under my stockings, one clever finger snapping them up, sliding along the leather of my harness and stroking my dick. My pussy ached and throbbed. With each pump the base of the cock abraded my clit, sending spasms of desire through me. I clenched my fingers into tight little fists and tried to arch my back against her hands but she stopped completely. Chastised, I sat quietly still for her and she rewarded me by continuing the exquisite torture.

'You need to powder your nose,' she said softly and I wasted no time in standing up and leaving the table.

The bathroom was tiled in soft rose and grey. Long, low benches sat about and the mirror reflected back my flushed and hectic face. I ran cold water over my wrists in an attempt to cool down but I was too excited. I headed for a stall, determined to take myself in hand, so to speak, when the door opened and Alex strolled in, a nasty grin on her handsome face.

Before I could say anything at all she swung me up on the counter, shoved my skirt up to my waist, and bent her head. Her mouth surrounded my flesh-coloured prick and her head bobbed. My hands tangled in her hair, turning her head to one side so that I could get a better view of her face as she sucked me off.

She stopped and backed up, that same smile on her face. 'That is a very big cock you have there, little girl, didn't anyone ever tell you that you are too little to play with things so big?'

My breath caught and exploded in a hard gasp of desire as her fingers undid my harness. She parted my legs, her fingers stroking the thin strip of my blonde pubic hair. The harness made a musical jangle as the buckles let go and she pulled the hard length of my cock away from the sticky opening of my pussy.

182

My hands drummed into the counter as she inserted my own dick into my wet slit. When it was all the way inside me she rubbed her fingers around my clit in tiny little circles for a brief moment, then she pulled me to my feet.

'So you want to wear your cock like a big girl, huh? Here's what you're going to do, you're going to wear it all right. Keep it nice and snug right there inside you.' She stuffed my harness into my purse and led me back to the table. I had to concentrate to hold my pussy shut; I was suddenly terrified that the thing would fall out and the few diners and the staff at the restaurant would see it. That fear intensified my desire to no end. I could feel slippery tendrils of fluid sliding down my legs.

Back at the table she ordered dessert, an opulent and creamy light confection. She spooned it into my mouth and her fingers pressed against my clit. 'Squeeze that hard dick inside you,' she said softly and I did. With every mouthful my pussy grew wetter, hotter. My lips were distended over that heavy and thick phallus; her fingers rubbed and circled and tickled and I could barely breathe. My hips began to move up and down and my eyes frantically scanned the place, wondering if anyone could see what we were doing, while a little part of me really didn't care if they did or not.

My pussy began to clench and open faster. I could not control myself any more; I began to swing my hips a bit faster, my mouth open for another bite of dessert. The cock was grinding almost painfully against my walls, bumping my cervix and driving me crazy with the need to come.

She bit my neck, just a tiny and slight little nip, and I came. Sticky juices flowed out of my pussy and onto the skirt of my dress and Alex chuckled as her fingers stroked the hard, swollen bud of my clit, eliciting tiny little aftershocks from me.

She cuddled me close to her side for a few minutes before releasing me. I took my purse and went back to the bathroom to try to clean up the mess and stow my stuff. The sticky white spot on the back of my dress was large and noticeable. I wiped at it with handfuls of hand towels but it did no good at all. Alex strolled in, her jacket over her arm. She held it out to me wordlessly and I put it on, enjoying the smell of her cologne on its lapel.

The night had fallen across the streets. From the busier avenues came the roar and rush of traffic and the glare of bright lights, but on the street where we stood it was fairly quiet. 'Would you like to walk or catch a cab?'

'I could walk.'

I regretted that almost instantly; every step brought a painful twinge from my vagina. After a few steps I began to actually enjoy that small pain. I had the whimsical thought that my body was attempting to hold onto a memory. My purse hung on my arm, the weight of the harness and dick pushing it out of its usual shape.

I wasn't sure what to say. What do you say to someone you just let fuck you at the dinner table? Thanks? The blocks unwound under our feet and we stopped in front of the brownstone in which I lived.

'I – I … don't usually … I mean, I don't generally wear that to dinner. I was nervous.' I blurted out. 'I hate blind dates as a rule.'

'Yeah, me too, but this one was a very memorable experience.' Her grey eyes gleamed as she lowered her face, her lips almost touching mine. 'I think we should do it again.'

'Me too. You have my number?'

'Yes, and you have mine.'

She sealed my mouth shut with a long kiss, took her jacket back, then opened the door and guided me through it. She waved goodbye and I stood on the stairs looking out the glass door at her lean body walking away before heading upstairs to my apartment.

Carrie looked up from a bag of chips as I walked in. 'Well, you weren't gone long enough to get laid so I guess it wasn't that good,' she said, going back to her magazine.

I stifled giggles at that comment. 'It was a very good dinner. A very, very good dinner.'

I went into my bedroom and stripped off my soiled dress. Just as I was stepping into the hot water my phone beeped and a text appeared on the screen. It read, *Lunch tomorrow?*

I would love to, I typed back. *I am a hungry girl.*

Me too, she wrote and I laughed as I got into the shower and started planning what I would wear to lunch.

Heating the Sauna
by Kathleen Tudor

'Again!' Nikki kneels over me, yelling encouragement, and I gasp, sweat dripping down my face, and obey. 'Yes! Just like that. Keep going!'

'Are you fucking kidding me?'

'Don't swear. Up!'

I take a big gulp of air, swear in my mind, just to be contrary, and lift the large stability ball clamped between my feet. As soon as it is above my hips I release, lowering it carefully and tightening my abs to raise it again. If that doesn't sound hard to you, try three sets of twenty at the end of an hour workout. My face is twisted into a grimace that makes Nikki grin, and I silently swear again. Nikki laughs, and I think she must have heard me.

The ball comes up for a third time and Nikki stands and grabs it in one smooth movement, just in time to prevent me from bouncing it across the room as I collapse. 'Nice job! How do your arms feel? I think we can add some weight to a few of those triceps lifts.'

'I hate you,' I mutter, unable to muster the energy to pry my eyes open.

'And yet you keep coming back. You must love that ass I've helped you carve out,' she teases.

'Don't swear,' I remind her, but I'm grinning, giddily happy that she's noticed how tight and round my ass has looked lately. She snorts and then goes to put the exercise ball away, and I tap into my reserves to get one eye open wide enough to check out my trainer's backside. I've gotta say, this alone is almost worth the pain of our weekly sessions.

I'd first started working out with Nikki three months ago, when I spotted her training some other hapless victim. I'd fallen for her adorable little pigtails – which at the time had been blonde shot through with streaks of pink – not to mention the body. She was tight and toned all over, and a relatively tiny woman, but so intimidating in the gym that no one would ever make the mistake of calling her delicate. Cute, however …

'See you next week?' Nikki asks as she reaches down to give me a hand up. I let her haul me to my feet, and feel recovered enough to pick up the yoga mat myself and drop it on the stack.

'If I don't drop dead in the meantime.' It's what I always say, and I'm pleased when I get the regular smile in return. Nikki has a dimple on her left cheek that makes me feel weak in the knees, although after what she's put me through today I'm already feeling sort of wobbly. She leans forward, gives me a hug, sweat and all, and breezes past me with her clipboard. I watch her leave, enjoying the view before I gather my towel and water bottle and head to the locker room.

I work out on my day off so that I can take the entire day for myself. Today that means a quick rinse in the shower, then wrapping myself in a towel and hitting the sauna. For some reason the room is always abandoned, but it's one of the things that drew me to this gym. I love lying back on the wooden bench in that dim room and letting the heat bake the sweat and (theoretically) the impurities out of my body. A half hour or more in that atmosphere, followed by a cool shower, always leaves me feeling energetic for days afterward.

I spread my towel on the bench of the sauna and stretch my naked body out, letting the heat creep into my pores. I open my mouth and breathe in deeply, letting the warmth get inside me too.

A few moments later I am starting to slip into the meditative state that the sauna brings to me, when I hear the door open and feel a rush of cool air. I sit halfway up, startled, and see Nikki standing in the doorway looking equally surprised to see me.

I very firmly command my eyes to remain on her face, and they gleefully disobey, skipping over her breasts (which are as taut as the rest of her), and resting on the closely cropped triangle of blonde hair between her legs. When I wrench my eyes back to her face, I can see that Nikki has noticed me noticing.

'No pink. I could have sworn that was natural,' I hear myself say, and if I wasn't already flushed from the heat, I would have blushed then.

Nikki breaks into a huge grin. 'I have a good stylist,' she says. 'I thought I was the only one who ever used the sauna.'

'It's my favourite way to unwind.'

'Me too. I usually bake a while after I've finished all of my appointments.'

I raise my eyebrows; my appointment was relatively early in the day. 'You're off early, then.'

'I had a couple of cancellations,' she says. As she's been speaking, she's been making her way slowly closer to me and I realise that I am still raised up on one elbow, sprawled across the bench like a Renaissance painting of a sex goddess. I feel the tingle of my cheeks trying frantically to blush – again – and start to sit up.

Nikki reaches out and rests a hand on my shoulder, freezing me in place. Her skin is cool against mine, not yet heated by the scorching air, but her touch is like fire shooting through me. She's touched me before, of course, and I've fantasised plenty, but this is different. I'm naked. She's naked. She's seen me looking. And she's still here, touching me.

My heart is about to pound through my throat and I don't know what to say, so I let my mouth off the leash. It comes up with, 'Are you gay?'

'No,' Nikki says thoughtfully, and my heart takes a U-turn and heads for my stomach, 'but I'm not straight either.' I swallow hard and wonder if the yo-yo routine is actually bad for my heart, seeing as it's back in my throat again. 'Is that good enough?'

I laugh, although it comes out sounding pretty choked. 'No problem; I've been picturing you naked since we first met.' Crap. Maybe it's time to take the mouth off of autopilot.

Fortunately, Nikki laughs, sounding delighted, and her hand moves over my shoulder and up behind my neck, caressing. 'And here I thought you were just committed to fitness,' she says. Her fingers burrow into my hair, and I tip back into the sensation for a moment before leaning forward and fulfilling a personal fantasy – I place a gentle kiss on her lips, and Nikki's hand tightens in my hair.

She pulls back and rakes me with hungry eyes. 'Are you cold?' she asks with a teasing lilt, and I see that my nipples are standing erect.

'Maybe –' I start to say, and my voice catches. I cough. 'Maybe you should come keep me warm.' Maybe autopilot isn't so bad after all.

Nikki's grin is almost predatory as she climbs up to straddle me. She sits on my hips, leaning forward over me. My entire body breaks out in aroused goosebumps.

'I am going to be so fired if anyone sees this.'

I grin back and trace a finger along her collarbone, watching her nipples rise to mirror mine. 'Good thing no one ever comes in here.'

'Good thing,' she repeats, and then she kisses me. She tastes like cinnamon, and I hum soft approval and dip my tongue into the warmth of her mouth to get a deeper taste. Our bodies press together, already slicked with sweat from the heat, and I wriggle, loving the slip of our breasts against one another. Hers are a handful and a little extra, firm and perky despite the fact that she's close to my own 32 years. Mine are larger, softer, and maybe a little less perky, but I've been told that they're perfect for a good grope. Nikki reaches up to give one a squeeze and purrs her approval into my mouth, and I smile into the kiss and arch up to encourage her.

Slowly I begin to sit up, pushing back into the kiss until we are completely upright with Nikki kneeling over my lap. 'I think it's my turn to give you orders for once,' I say, and a hitch in her breath precedes a pleased smile.

'Think you can handle me?'

Instead of answering, I hunch forward and lift one of her gorgeous breasts to nip at the nipple. She gives a yip that sounds half surprised, half pleased, but she doesn't move away. 'I've been dreaming of how your cunt would taste since the first time I saw you,' I say. 'Lie down.'

Nikki laughs, but she complies, moving back to lie down in the space between my legs. Seconds later I am crouched at the juncture of her thighs. I inhale deeply, and the hot, dry air carries the scent of her to me in an intoxicating wave. I savour the sensations that ripple through me as a result, and prolong the moment, turning my head to taste the sweat on her muscular thighs rather

191

than diving into my ultimate goal.

Her legs are like a dancer's, all long, lean muscle. I run my tongue across the curve of one thigh and feel her muscles quiver in reaction. She is salty, drenched in sweat from the furnace heat of the sauna, and I lick again, savouring the taste.

'You smell amazing,' I say, making sure my breath stirs the hot air against her pussy. She grunts but doesn't speak. 'I bet you taste even better.' She growls this time, balling my towel in her fists. I laugh, and she growls again. 'What, are you in a hurry?' And then, when she isn't expecting it, I let my tongue dart forward to taste the nectar between her lips. Nikki lets out a strangled cry and bucks her hips up toward me, but I've already moved back. 'That's a nice view,' I say. 'Lift your hips up. Hold them there …'

'You are playing with fire,' Nikki says, but she obeys, bringing her heels toward her ass and lifting her hips up until her pussy is raised up and displayed before. I accept the offering by cupping her ass and bringing my face into her, plunging my tongue in deep. Her muscles tense and shake all over as she struggles to come quietly, and although I am shocked at how quickly and easily she's come for me, I do my part to make it difficult to stay silent, tonguing her eagerly.

When she quiets down I lean back. 'You've got a hairpin trigger,' I say.

It takes Nikki another moment to gather herself. 'So I do,' she says.

She's left her hips raised up for me, so I lift one hand and part her damp, shining folds. Nikki whimpers in pleasure, then she moans as I slide my fingers inside her. I pump slowly, keeping carefully clear of Nikki's sensitive clit. It is gorgeous, the way she offers up her slick body to me, trembling with the effort of staying lifted. I watch the contortions of her face as her pleasure builds again, and just as her eyes squeeze shut and she reaches for climax I give her that extra push, leaning in to suck her clit into my mouth and stroke it with my tongue.

Nikki collapses, writhing, and thrusts a fist into her mouth to stop her screams of pleasure. Her clit is ripped away from my mouth but my hand follows her down and I pump hard now, following the crest of her orgasm and driving her even higher. She starts to come down again, but almost immediately her muffled cries change pitch and I grin hungrily as she comes again, the convulsions around my fingers renewing as she continues to squirm and buck against me.

'Wow, you're so lucky,' I murmur, slowing my pace and allowing her to calm.

'Makes it hell to keep a straight face on a bike,' she jokes back, but she is still panting and there is a bite mark on her hand. I slide my fingers free and move myself over her, taking her bitten hand into my mouth to kiss the place she'd used to smother the sounds of her pleasure.

'I bet.' And then something occurs to me. 'You ride a motorcycle.' It's hard to tell with her face already flushed and red from the heat and the orgasms, but I'm pretty sure she blushes. I laugh with delight and kiss her deeply. She cups the back of my head and manages to roll us over so that she is on top of me on the narrow bench.

'Now it's payback,' she says, and I part my legs happily as she positions herself between them.

Nikki doesn't tease. Her tongue laps all the way up my slit – which is practically dripping with arousal after watching her come – and then finds my nub. She licks and tastes for a moment, then latches on and suckles gently. 'Oh God,' I moan, trying to stay as quiet as possible. It

193

has been a while since I've been so damned turned on, and my body is exquisitely sensitive. I am already soaring with pleasure when she penetrates me, finger-fucking me in time with her mouth's ministrations. I'm already writhing against her and biting the back of my own hand to keep my whimpers quiet, so I don't quite scream when she crooks her fingers and sends my orgasm crashing through me like a tidal wave.

My ears actually ring with the echoes of that intense pleasure and I pant hard to catch my breath. When I have to strength to look up, Nikki is licking my cream from her fingers with a satisfied smirk on her face. I laugh as I grab her wrist and pull her down to kiss me, tasting my own sweet tang on her tongue.

'Am I going to pay for this at our next session?' I ask.

'You bet.'

'You at least going to make it up to me?'

'Maybe … But it might be better to do it somewhere less … risky. My place?'

'Depends. Can we take the bike?'

It was definitely a blush. Nikki kisses me one last time, gently pulling at my hair to force a pleased whimper out of me, then she releases me and leaves the room with one last wink over her shoulder. 'See you next week.'

The Silent Observer
by Alcamia Payne

Kitten had had a man in her room last night, Bella thought as, resting her plump legs on the railing, she gazed down into the courtyard. There was no getting away from the fact. The man had come early and Bella had crept to the edge of the balcony to watch the impetuous displays of tango and bossa nova – her jealousy rising with each metronomic jounce of their hips.

Of course Kitten entertained men, why shouldn't she? Typically French, she was beautiful, with a heart-shaped face surrounded by a casque of jet black hair and full, pouting lips she painted in rich cunt-dripping carmine lipstick. She couldn't have been better named either. *Kitten;* tiny, mystical, slinky and, to top it all off, with a purring voice that made Bella shiver.

Bella had never had an obsession; however, she realised early on she had an unhealthy interest in Kitten. It had started the day Bella moved in and Kitten, who'd been watering the geraniums on her windowsill and who'd been dressed in a skimpy bikini, had smiled at her. Bella, startled, shrunk back behind the shutters her heart pumping. She wasn't sure what she'd just set eyes on but she felt like she'd been run over by a truck and her whole body oozed energy; the kind of tingling sexual energy she'd experienced only once before.

Naturally, she stood no chance with this petite feline

and that had been made clear to her early on. The Polish girl who lived upstairs had said to Bella, 'Why, that's Kitten Dupré, they say she's a siren. Everyone goes mad about her. She had a chance in a movie with a famous director but she fell in love with the leading lady and he became vindictive and left her penniless, effectively destroying her career. That's why she now coaches dance and voice.'

'How terrible,' Bella said, a queer sensation circulating in the pit of her stomach. 'Poor little Kitten.'

Kitten also adored women. She'd sit sipping coffee at the corner café, her gently curving eyes appraising, her pouty lips opening and closing in a daring invitation of sex every time she saw a rounded butt, narrow ankle, or pair of pertly erect nipples. Somehow this made it worse for Bella, who could have tolerated Kitten's desire for a man but not the direct competition of a female. The fact Kitten was a lesbian brought her dangerously close to Bella's orbit. She was a possibility, but only barely that – since a girl like Kitten would never look at Bella. No, that would be ridiculous. Kitten was a tiny little thing and Bella was 5 foot 11, came from Buenos Aires, and was, as Mario was always keen to point out, slightly larger than your average woman.

Bella frowned as unwelcome thoughts trickled through her consciousness like water through a crack. Most of them were due to Mario. Mario owned the deli which was beneath the apartments and he really dug Bella. Whenever she came down the stairs he'd lean against the door and make lewd pussy-sucking sounds and filthy comments under his breath whilst blocking her way with his huge, sweaty body. These comments made Bella – who was unsure of her extraordinary allure – wonder why men should lust after her when she was such a tall, corpulent women. Stripping naked, she observed her body from every possible angle in her large mirror and couldn't for the life of her locate the key to her desirability. Largeness ran in her genes. Both her mother and grandmother had been big women. Bella's largeness, though, had recently assumed mammoth proportions and effectively swallowed up any logical perception of herself so she couldn't clearly see her other qualities any more. Notably, her sexy demeanour, sleek, black hair, almond-shaped, luminous eyes, and velvet soft, café au lait skin. There was no easy way to say it. Mario's comments made her feel worse and she scrubbed off her lipstick and ordered a new uniform two sizes too large, to hide her voluptuousness.

Kitten moved silently about the flat, hugging the shadows like her namesake and springing out as if pouncing on a ball of wool whenever she saw Bella. When she smiled, Bella melted internally and her female orifices joyfully exuded in juicy anticipation. When she spoke, Bella took a step or two back or even darted for cover. Kitten must have thought she was very strange indeed.

One day Kitten caught her red-handed, her casque of hair and grin emerging from behind her own shutters with the stealth of a cat stalking a mouse. 'I hear you're a dancer too? An expert in rumba?'

'Once, yes,' Bella replied.

'Dancing is so sexy.' Kitten pressed her finger to her lips. 'You know, I'm a dancer too, it would be such fun to work together, to dance together. What do you think?'

Bella had to act quickly. 'I don't have time and I'm between jobs and … I think this will disappoint you. I'm now a maid at an international hotel.' She was trapped by invisible claws, but the paws concealing the claws were soft velvet and she was reluctant to go. She hovered tremulously, as if caught in a magnetic force field. On the one hand she'd give anything to speak to the object of her lusts and let that sexy purr fuck her all over. On the other hand she was terrified of allowing herself so much uninhibited bliss. It was difficult, but she retreated into the shadows determined not to let such a pounce – claws out – happen again.

The result now was Bella hid from Kitten and became a secret observer. Lips pressed to the shutters, her body became a badly behaved piece of biological machinery which moistened and quickened when she didn't want it to. Her thoughts directing her movements, she began to do naughty things, her hands slithering down between her legs to caress the plump, shaved skin which Bella kept fragranced and oiled in the hope – yes, the slim hope – it might one day be kissed and teased by feminine lips. She shouldn't surrender. However, she did constantly. She would tease open a button or two of her straining top to experimentally squeeze her rounded breasts with their prominent erect nipples, the most rigid of which sported one great concession – a real diamond nipple stud.

Bella rapidly found herself pulled into the orbit of Kitten and she began to do more and more daring things. After all, she conceded, what was the harm? The stunning girl remained an object of adoration although she'd never possibly seduce her. She dragged her old armchair closer to the shutters and, with legs splayed, she began a studied art of seduction as, watching Kitten, she stroked first her thigh and then ventured closer to the warm, wet place between her legs with its clipped Mohican tuft.

Bella, who often masturbated frantically in front of her enormous antique mirror, was next struck by an idea. When Kitten went out to work, she situated the mirror at a cunning angle between the wall and the balcony. Bella could be devious when it suited her, and she was thrilled to discover that on the occasions when Kitten's balcony doors were thrown wide open the reflections from both the glass and the mirror gave her a wonderful tripartite view of Kitten's bohemian apartment. The shock made Bella sit down with a thump. It was quite a surprise because Kitten was really a queen of the jungle and inhabited a lavishly appointed, eccentric boudoir with lots of sexy things: trailing voiles, seductive erotic prints, jungle wallpaper, and smoothly rounded statues. The sight of it made Bella's blood rush. Never had she encountered such a shady haven of dark, sensual taboo.

They were in the midst of a heatwave, and one day Bella sat in the shadows dabbing a cologne-scented hankie over her ripples of flesh as she hitched her voluptuous thigh over the chair arm. She'd rolled her favourite silk robe up to her waist and was flapping it to permit what little breeze there was to feather her skin. It had become as hot as the inside of an oven and virtually impossible to keep cool in her little apartment.

Bella sat up with a start, her eyes widening in surprise. Her finely tuned antennae had detected that Kitten had entered the apartment and switched on the radio, but this was totally out of character. She was generally at work at this time of the day. Bella's cheeks flushed as she angled herself to gaze in the mirror. Kitten, who was dressed in black ballet pumps and skin-tight pants, was standing right in the centre of the room unbuttoning her black blouson. Letting it drop, she caught it with her toe and flicked it onto the floor. The vision of her alabaster skin and two pert upturned breasts with their stubbornly erect nipples made the silent observer breathless with lust. But it was what dangled from them which most surprised

Bella. Kitten wore nipple clamps between which hung a thin gold chain, and on the chain, threatening to tug down those delicious little teats, was a sparkling fake diamond droplet.

To make matters worse Kitten was smiling and wriggling her body in tune with a song on the radio, the stunning skin-tight pants inching down centimetre by tantalizing centimetre.

Bella, who still had her thumb deep within her wet slit, was surprised to find she was turned to stone. Having jerked down the pants, Kitten angled away, presenting her buttocks, which were as pert and alabaster white as her breasts and which flowed seamlessly into toned and sinuous dancer's legs.

Once, when Bella had been young, she'd had a lover who had also been a dancer; a South American – a tall, masculine woman with skin the colour of ebony and sweetly pouting lips, and yet a savagery about her which made Bella feel safe. Yes, curiously, Bella was totally at home with aggression and direction rather than this soft, kittenish seduction. It was as if the forward thrust of aggression in the woman had enabled her to compete somehow with her size. She'd been content to be propelled around the floor in a pair of strong female arms which had the tensile strength of a man. There had been a frosting of manly hair on the woman's top lip and she'd smelt of male heat and cologne. She couldn't have been more different to Kitten, whose wafts of expensive floral perfume reached Bella even here. The idea of holding, indeed of seducing such exquisite feminine beauty melted Bella's insides. It was no good; she was totally in this enchantress's thrall, and yet in just an instant of seeing perfection her dream seemed further away.

Slithering down and squinting through the crack in the

shutter, Bella spied the glint of something ten times more exciting than the first revelation. It was another thin slither of chain which dangled from the girl's cunt and which she was now winding thoughtfully around her finger as her glance darted here and there before seeming to meet Bella's in the mirror, drilling into her.

Bella folded her robe around her ample hips self-consciously, as if by so doing she might disappear, but Kitten, who was now provocatively sucking her lip, sashayed closer, like an oriental cat or maybe a panther. She was exquisite even down to her tiny, suckable toes. This made it harder for Bella, who had seduced her so many times in her mind her entire body flushed crimson at the memory and she began to vibrate like a latent volcano. Turned to stone, she was too scared to move as the object of her affections proceeded to squat down and, getting down on her belly, wriggled closer to the balcony door so she could press her eye to the slats. Kitten's petulant, rouged lips opened so she could flick out her pink tongue and tickle the wood with a suggestive motion. By a dint of fate it was as if she knew where Bella had situated the mirror, and she proceeded to extend first one leg, exposing the slit of her cunt and trickling her hand down in a musical arpeggio of innuendo, and then the other. With a mewl of passion, she fell onto her back and, writhing and contorting her limbs like a sea creature, began to seduce herself with more panache than a man ever could. First, her dainty hands smoothed over her tiny breasts, jerking frantically on the chain as they did so, then they came down and separated her cunt, so Bella was treated to the delectable sight of Kitten's juicy, roseate folds and disproportionately large clitoris, which had been so well trained by the weight of the chain it was swollen and trembled as it was pinched and rotated between

201

Kitten's thumb and forefinger. The feline creature continued to squeal and jerk as her orgasm exploded and kept on exploding. Something almost purely metaphysical reached out and touched Bella, making her own body shudder and convulse in resonance as the brush of her robe on her nipples precipitated that rarest of things, a gut-wrenching spontaneous climax.

Kitten was certainly a steamy little thing, with these impromptu theatricals becoming a regular occurrence. In a storm of unrequited love, Bella made certain she was well prepared for each show by applying her own nipple clamps and pushing her butt dildo firmly into place whilst pushing her vibrator high up inside her as far as it would go. Next, she'd lie still as a statue and observe the cavorting of her illicit lover.

The following week, Bella was mortified to see Kitten stroll into the apartment with a woman. To be truthful, she experienced such a violent stab of jealousy that for an instant her heart seemed to stop beating. Only one shaded lamp shone in Kitten's boudoir and the two women were a seductive tableau as they pressed against one another. Bella watched, open-mouthed, as Kitten, having procured a blindfold, placed it over the woman's eyes and then proceeded to seduce her by unbuttoning her clothes, dropping to her knees, and treating her to a languid tongue bath. The odd thing was Bella realised it was she who was being seduced, each touch of that finger and tongue having a powerful and instantaneous effect on her. Eventually, Kitten's head vanished between the woman's corpulent legs, which Bella saw with satisfaction were not shaped half as nicely as her own. It was very disturbing being the witness to such wanton, and in a manner, sexual duplicity, and Bella clapped her hand to her mouth, her passion snuffed out like a candle flame as the betrayal bit fiercely, because betrayal it was. Kitten might not have known about her personally; however, by now there had been so many observations in seduction Bella felt she knew every inch of her lover's kittenish body.

Forced to watch, she chewed her lip as the statuesque woman fastened a ludicrous strap-on around her waist and fucked Kitten from behind whilst Kitten, her head buried in her arms, made no sound at all as her petite body jerked and the impossibly big thing worked in and out.

Bella was mysteriously affected by what she'd witnessed and, despite the fact the only breath of wind came from her propped-open door, she locked herself away and spent the sweltering summer nights sprawled on her bed. Unrequited love was a terrible thing; the saving grace – yes, the only hope on reflection – that Kitten appeared to favour women who were larger and more voluptuous than average. Not that that helped Bella, who thought she'd never be able to look her in the face again. She buried her face in her pillow and her body shuddered with despair. Finally, unable to bear the heat any longer, she crept to the door and propped it open. She seemed fairly safe, she mused, as, with a sigh of pleasure, she fanned her red cheeks with her hands. Kitten couldn't seem to care less. The evening breeze wound up the ancient staircase and fluttered over her skin, and Bella, her tanned, lustrous skin glistening with the barest suggestion of fragranced perspiration, plopped back down on her bed and promptly fell asleep.

She woke with a start. A sound had disturbed her. 'Shit,' she murmured; someone was in her room. Well, it was her fault. Opening the door like that had been a stupid thing to do. She sat up, her large breasts wobbling as the shadow came closer and closer still until Kitten – since that was who she now saw it was – bent over her and slithered onto the bed, her lips a fraction away from hers. Kitten sat in the darkness, her skin alabaster in the spool of light from the moon as she hugged her skinny knees. She was dressed in a tiny black dress, one strap of which had fallen from her shoulder, revealing a tantalizing tit, and which was so rucked up around her butt Bella could see her crotch.

'Bella, I wondered if you were ill. Where have you been? You weren't avoiding me, were you? I thought we were friends.'

'Why the hell would I avoid you?' Bella chuckled, but it was a chuckle without a great deal of conviction.

Kitten stroked her hair back behind her ears and it was then Bella noticed her eyes seemed to be glistening with tears. Before she had a chance to move, Kitten stretched out beside her and Bella quivered as she experienced the tiny bones and energetic body squeezed passionately against her. As much as she tried to deny it, she was burning with excitement.

'What does a girl have to do?' Kitten continued, her hand trickling down Bella's plump arm and over her hand, where it stroked with metronomic movements. 'How obvious did I have to make it?'

'Make what?' Bella croaked.

Kitten was leaning so close her breath was warm on Bella's cheek. She smelt of lavender pastille and a fragrant heady soap. *'Tu fais la bêtise.* You're being silly and hiding from me.'

Bella raised an eyebrow at this comment.

'It isn't as if I didn't know you fancied me. Of course you do, playing that silly game.' Kitten grinned and out darted her pink tongue. She ran it across Bella's lips with excruciating slowness. 'Such silly games, *chérie*. Did you think I wouldn't see you? Always you are watching. A silent observer. I see you every day, half-hidden behind your shutters as if you're waiting for the next instalment in a play.'

Bella blinked. Once she'd watched a fly trapped in a window as it battered itself helplessly on the glass. There had been no escape and this was exactly how she was feeling now. None of this could be happening. She was dreaming, wasn't she?

Exactly at that instant, Kitten fell on Bella and began tracing her fingers over her face. Bella hardly dared breathe for fear of breaking the enchanting spell. She felt desperately inadequate as her mind rampaged backwards in time to her graphic daydreams of writhing bed scenes. Oh, damn her impulses. Why couldn't she control her body's torrid craving for female sex? Down between her legs things were happening, things beyond her control; her body was becoming warmer and positively fizzing with energy. Kitten's finger's danced around her large breasts, palpating here and there. A tiny squeeze, a pinch, then out darted Kitten's tongue and she was lapping. No, not just lapping, nibbling with her tiny teeth, tugging this way and that, often quite violently. Bella moaned and Kitten glided further down her body, snuffling her belly and jumping astride Bella's hips and moving back and forth. Holding Bella open with her hands, she ground her pubes mercilessly into her.

Enraptured, all Bella could do was watch Kitten, who, with arms raised above her head, kept twisting her agile body this way and that. It was pale perfection, all waving limbs and tight, clenching muscles beyond the confines of the little black dress. Bella's heart beat faster and in tune with the bouncing pocket dynamo. Her hips were trying to punch upwards to give herself the satisfaction she required. As Kitten inserted her thumb cleverly inside her hole and found a heavenly place which sent Bella writhing out of control, those hips thrust convulsively, almost unseating her lover. Tensing her buttocks, Bella bit her lip and, with a gasp of such pleasure, gave into a moment's orgasmic bliss. Kitten was older than Bella had first thought, she reflected. Up close and personal, the face possessed a serious beauty, and the odd frown line added a daring sophistication. Bella writhed on the bed, unable to get enough of the kisses which were deep and delicious and interspersed with both of their touching tongues dancing and marrying together, then drawing apart in a tango of seduction.

Suddenly, Kitten jumped off the bed. 'Come, it's so much cooler in my apartment. Yours is like Monsieur Fourier's bread oven.'

Kitten wove her fingers through Bella's and, before she knew it, Bella was hypnotised and following in her wake, through the door and into the boudoir; the jungle of shades she'd espied so many times and from which Kitten often peeped, making those lurid kissing motions with lips and tongue.

Bella sat down heavily on a bed festooned by voile curtains. In a sense it was a relief to surrender, although the mystery of the encounter had been destroyed and surely the furtive and illicit nature of her dreams would crumble and die. The reality of sex rarely lived up to its expectations.

Bella trembled, sitting with her hands sandwiched beneath her thighs, her body vibrating, mouth open in an "o" of enjoyment as her large, pink nipples rose stridently to attention and goosebumps exploded in a parade across her skin. Kitten stood posed with her back to her. The dress had slipped, exposing the sweet curve of a shoulder, and Bella, breathless with expectation, watched the fabric slide further still. The girl executed the perfect striptease, exposing each snowy inch of flesh while letting the dress cling cunningly to every angle. Head turned slightly to one side, Bella was struck once more by how perfectly feline Kitten was, with the arched pussy back and her black lashes which owned nothing to the mascara bottle. Heavens! Kitten held the dress to her hips, vacillating a moment before letting it go further to reveal her pert pair of buttocks, as tight and perfectly rounded as Bella had fantasised from a distance, and which were covered in a tease of lace; the smallest, thinnest pair of black panties imaginable. With a rustle, the dress completed its descent and Kitten raised one elegant leg at a time and flipped off her shoes as she turned around.

'You're the biggest tease,' she purred, coming to stand in front of Bella and putting her hands on her cheeks. Bella screwed the bedsheets in her fists as paroxysms of passion took over. Her head was spinning. Kitten was so perfect, so gorgeous, and the two tight, pert breasts, little larger than half an orange and surmounted by what she now saw were extravagant hennaed nipples, were pressed against her skin. Bella sighed. Kitten's smooth belly invited a kiss. Bella grabbed her hips. Pulling her close, planted a kiss right on her navel as she tugged down the lace panties. Kitten squealed but squeezed closer so Bella was overcome by her sweet feminine muskiness and heat. Oh, she was so tempting there; smooth and rounded, the perfect slit juicy and inviting. Bella inserted her thumb with its silver thumb ring and Kitten shuddered in delight.

'I wanted you for so long, why did you play with me?' Kitten stroked Bella's lush hair and loosened it from its combs so it fell in black ripples across her shoulders.

'You played with me,' Bella riposted huskily, burying her mouth in the fragrant, musky heat and licking the warm moist rises and falls; tickling and jabbing here and there with the tip of her tongue.

'I acted out the things I dreamed of actually doing with you. However, I began to lose hope,' Kitten retorted.

Before she could stop her, Kitten had gone, darting to her wardrobe to take out the strap-on. Dropping to her knees, she tugged off Bella's robe and licked Bella all over. It took ages, and by the time the anxious little tongue was between her legs Bella was ready to explode. With her neat little claws Kitten scratched her delicate undulations and Bella tossed and turned as one orgasmic explosion after another detonated.

Later, she wrapped her corpulent arms around her lover and felt the bones shudder.

'You're so soft, Bella,' Kitten cooed. 'I always prefer a larger woman, I like to be lost within the softness, and it's erotic to feel smothered. Fuck me,' she ordered, holding up the strap-on.

Bella wanted to, but as she began to buckle up she felt a little reluctance, wondering if she would crush the delicate kitten bones. Then she recalled the dancer, and her adversary certainly had not hurt her feline conquest. Kitten rose up on her haunches, holding open her plump sex slit. She was such a tease and Bella, with a growl like a tiger, lunged forward, thrusting the tool between Kitten's now raised and waving legs. The legs locked around her and Kitten's scent swept up and over her in an evocative cloud as tiny claws drew her down. Bella took the nipple chain in her teeth, angling her head to one side. She was surprised there was an artfully positioned mirror in the apartment, and what was most delightful was that it was angled so she could watch as she buried herself deeply between those tight thighs.

Kitten purred and pistoned insatiably, and the strap-on's reverse end rubbed pleasurably in just the right places to give Bella another orgasm.

She trailed her hand over Kitten's damp skin as the girl lay purring and cushioned on her plump breasts. She was smiling.

'Shit, you perv, didn't you think I knew?'

'Knew what?' Bella asked candidly.

'You'd been watching me and I'd been watching you, for ages.' Kitten smirked. 'I placed one little mirror there on my mantle and I angled it to look into my cheval. The reflection gives me an excellent view into your mirror so I can see everything you do – and you do the naughtiest things.' She smoothed her thigh up and down Bella's as she licked her lips. 'Did you enjoy my little show?'

Bella drew back. 'What show?'

'My, my, *ma chérie*. The one I put on for you with Dahlia, of course.' Kitten stared at her. 'Bella, you're not about to cry are you?'

'Cry, why should I cry?' Bella retorted sharply. 'So, you entertained a woman?'

'But, not just any woman.' Kitten moved one leg over her belly so her wet crotch was rubbing her lover's. She jiggled the chain, tugging her nipples into peaks. 'It was Dahlia who freed me.' She pressed her mouth to Bella's, and Bella enjoyed the flickering tongue as Kitten made saucy kissing motions. 'But, I don't in any way love her. It's impossible to love Dahlia. I wanted to make you jealous, you see. I'd had such naughty fantasies about you for so long, wondering how I could get you to loosen up.' Her voice dropped an octave or two. 'I watched you, watched you very carefully all the time I fucked Dahlia and Dahlia fucked me and I was wondering how my strap-on would feel coming onto me with your ample curves pumping.' Her dazzling stare pinned Bella like a fly and her mouth hung open, as if in the act of being fucked from a distance. 'Now.' Kitten crooked her finger. 'I think this whole fiasco's over at last.'

Pinning Bella's arms to the bed, Kitten clambered onto her soft flesh and ground her body over Bella's as sensuously as any Siamese cat. Then, as she sat astride and lowered herself onto the strap-on, Bella moved her hands over the silky soft skin and pressed her lips to perfumed perfection. Kitten was completely shaved, with not one hair to mar her perfection. She was quite the most perfect thing Bella had ever seen.

Kitten took her hand and kissed it as she began to move up and down. Bella was soon to learn she could take a great deal of fucking as she swivelled around and bent over, presenting her perfect butt for Bella's rings and fat digits.

Bella was reminded of the kitten she'd owned a long time ago and which, coiled like a warm serpent in her lap, was always licking and caressing. Cats were capable of so much unconditional affection.

'Bella, I do adore you.'

Bella experienced a warm glow which spread all over her flesh until she became molten. In that moment, she realised Kitten truly did love her. Now, what an extraordinary thing that was.

Dressed to Impress
by Emma Lydia Bates

On Friday night my darling comes hurrying home. I'm pressed against the wall with her hands in my hair and her lips against mine and her breasts pressed against me before I've had a chance to say hello. Only by the time she's midway through pulling up my skirt, breathing, 'I missed you, Serena,' in my ear, do I remember to close the front door.

'Good day?' I ask her when she eventually lets me go. I catch a glance of myself in the mirror – my hair, which was neatly curled, now looks like a minor explosion on the top of my head, and I have to pull up my dress so that the lace edge of my bra isn't showing – but then I catch a glance of my darling, all red lips, bobbed hair and curves, and I have to kiss her all over again.

'*Good* day,' she says happily, catching my wrist and pulling me into the kitchen. 'Remember the tricky make-up job on the lead? We've figured out a way to make it work when we go on tour after Christmas.'

My darling works for a theatre group, and knows how to do everything under the sun – her dressing room once had a sign saying "Rose Corelli: General Dogsbody" – while I'm at home all day translating books, mostly recipe books, from French. She has intrigues among the cast to tell me about; I usually have odd ways that people have chosen to describe a perfectly cooked lobster to tell her about in return.

'And,' she adds, 'I have a great idea for what we're going to do tonight.'

I smile, and she reaches to tuck a ringlet of my hair behind my ear.

'Don't look so nervous,' she says.

If I do, it's unsurprising. Friday night is Date Night. Friday night is when my darling decides to raid the props cupboard and insist that we have sex in costume. As pirates. Or nurses. Or she wonders what it would be like to fuck someone while wearing infrared goggles. It's hard to get bored with her around.

'I want to go out with a boy tonight,' she announces.

Now that is surprising. My darling has known since she played with dolls that Barbie was hotter than Ken. She likes women, she likes *ladies*, with flowing dresses on slender figures, heels, and long hair that curls over the breasts, Lady Godiva style. She likes women who wouldn't be out of place in a pre-Raphaelite painting. She likes women, in short, like me.

Given she's the sexiest thing on Earth, I'm profoundly grateful.

'Where do you want me to get one of those from?' I ask.

She has a wicked grin from ear to ear. 'Sweetie,' she says, 'let's get down to business...'

She takes me by the hand and leads me to the bedroom. 'Strip,' she instructs.

When she's looking at me like that – warm eyes, wicked grin – it's impossible not to do what my darling tells me. I pull my dress over my head, and stand there in front of her, in my pale pink silk bra and matching knickers, both trimmed with lace, with a white lace suspender belt and white stockings besides. It's a set that she loves, and it always makes me feel like a princess when I wear it, especially when we light candles and scatter rose petals on the bed.

My darling snaps her fingers. 'Off with it,' she says. 'The lot.'

I hesitate for a moment, before I unhook my bra and suspender belt, and stand naked in front of her. My small breasts perk up with the cold. She traces one finger slowly over my nipple. I shiver, and reach to pull her towards me, but she steps back.

'Stay there,' she tells me.

I wait, feeling cold, feeling vulnerable.

It's not long before she returns with a small bag full of things. 'I stopped off at the shops on the way,' she says. 'I'm pretty sure these'll fit. Close your eyes.'

It feels a little bit like she's putting a climbing-wall harness on me, with straps under the curve of my bum and across the base of my back. She takes my hand and puts it on my crotch, and I can feel that she's strapped a dildo to me. It's not as hard as the ones we usually use. Then she tells me to open my eyes, and makes me put on boxer shorts too.

The effect, when I see myself in the mirror of my dressing table, verges on the obscene – flowing hair and breasts with soft pink nipples above, and the crotch of a half-hard young man below. It's so incongruous I laugh. My darling stands behind me, with one hand on my breast, and reaches into my boxers, underneath the harness, with the other, to caress my clitoris until I moan and relax against her, the delicious warmth of her body pressed against mine. But then she moves away again.

Stepping around me, she presses her face into my neck, then moves down to suck my nipples, each in turn.

She looks up and grins at me.

'Don't get too excited,' she says, 'we're going out tonight.'

Suddenly, as well as being turned on I'm intensely nervous – and more so when she nudges me to raise my arms and begins to wind bandages around my chest so my breasts are pressed flat, my erect nipples responding to the slight chafing of the cloth. With straps around my crotch and fabric pressing tightly on my nipples I begin to feel even more self-conscious, even more aroused.

My darling has me put on a man's shirt and jeans, and then sits me down at my dressing table. The dildo feels heavy between my legs; she's positioned it so it's not immediately obvious, but I'm furiously conscious that any wrong movement and it will look obscene. Of course, that's exactly how she intends it.

Looking in the mirror, I still look like a feminine woman – albeit a flat-chested one – who's borrowed her boyfriend's clothes. But that doesn't last long. My darling is, among other things, a make-up artist. She pulls my hair back into a bun, and begins to do her best to turn me into a man. First, all the make-up I had on already is gently wiped away, and then a little shading makes my jaw look squarer. She thickens my eyebrows and disguises my cheekbones. There's not much she can do with my hair, but she musses it up, and draws it back into a ponytail, pulling different sections of it more so that my hairline looks less feminine. Then, with a stipple sponge, she dabs around my mouth and all of a sudden I have reasonably convincing stubble.

She puts her face next to mine and smiles at me in the mirror.

'See,' she says, 'I have a boyfriend now.'

I doubt I would convince anyone who looked at me for

214

more than a couple of minutes. But, at first glance, the effect is convincing enough.

There's something in me that wants to rebel. I put my hand between my legs and feel the hard weight of a cock there, and it feels fundamentally wrong to me. But my darling purrs in my ear and kisses my neck, and says, 'You look hot.' And then I do feel hot, I feel aroused and sexy and uncomfortable all at the same time, and I can deal with that in the safety of our bedroom where I can take off all the layers and transform myself into a woman again, but my darling is finding me socks and shoes, and telling me we should get going soon, she doesn't want to be out too late, and I feel a twinge of nerves.

We don't go far; just far enough that the bar we pick is one where we're not likely to be recognised. The bouncer doesn't give me a second look. In fact, what strikes me most of all is the complete lack of attention we're getting. My darling slaps my bum, and then, when we're got ourselves drinks and sat down, reaches between my legs and presses her hand over the bulge. That's when I discover that this particular dildo vibrates when you put pressure on it, and the other end of it is pressed firm against my clitoris. I only just manage to stop myself from moaning.

My darling giggles. 'Do you like it when I touch your cock?' she asks.

And with a hint of growing confidence, I nod.

The next hour or so passes in much the same way. As far as most of the people in the bar are concerned, we're a reasonably normal heterosexual couple, possibly a bit heavy on the PDA, needing to go home and fuck – but not remarkable. And all the time I can feel the heaviness of the fake cock in my jeans, my breasts bound flat with my nipples rubbing against the binding, and my darling sitting next to me, drinking in the theatre of sensations from what she's done to my body, loving the fact that no one knows but us. Every so often I start to relax a little, to get comfortable, and then she presses her hand against my cock and pleasure shoots along my clitoris and I feel that quiver of delicious deviance. What would the other people in here think if they knew what we were up to? What would they say? My darling ordered our drinks, so unless they heard my voice – which is close to a contralto anyway – there would be little to give us away. But there's still that thrill of fear that makes me feel even more aroused.

A barmaid comes over to collect our glasses. I have my arm around my darling, but the barmaid brushes against my hand when she collects my glass regardless, leaning over the table a little lower than is necessary, her breasts spilling out of her low-cut top.

I can't resist. 'Thanks, love,' I purr, and my darling, game for anything, winks at her for good measure.

Now she's not sure what to make of the two of us, but straightens up, tosses her hair a little, and smiles. 'Are you guys having a good time tonight?' she asks.

'A very good time,' I assure her. In monosyllables, I can keep my voice to a low rumble that's convincing enough.

She hesitates for a second, then, with deliberate emphasis, says, 'Let me know if there's *anything* I can do to improve it.'

'Oh, we will,' says my darling.

It's hard not to burst into giggles when the barmaid walks away, but my darling turns to me and her hand is between my legs again, and she's kissing me, hard, and though I've no idea what it feels like, I think this must be what it's like to have an erection, this firm need between my legs, my beautiful girlfriend by my side and a cute barmaid who wants to flirt with the both of us.

I almost drag my darling out of the bar when she says, 'How about we get you home?'

The walk home takes longer than usual – my darling pulls me into a side street, presses me against the wall and kisses me furiously, her hand deep in my jeans, and then I cover her cleavage with kisses until a taxi driver honks his horn and we pull apart, embarrassed. But even then we kiss at every traffic light. It's a testament to stage make-up that it isn't smudged all over my face – and when I catch sight of the two of us in a shop window, it's a shock yet again. There's a sexy, curvaceous woman and some scruffy, skinny guy with his hands all over her; it takes me a moment before I recognise the couple at all.

We spill into the landing and, laughing, my darling pulls me up the stairs behind her. I nearly fall over trying to kick off my shoes, but then we're on the bed and she's in my arms, her face in my neck. I can touch her properly and it's glorious. She sits astride me – rubbing against my crotch quite on purpose so that she pushes down on my cock and I tremble in delight – and pulls off her jumper, letting her full, creamy breasts spill out in her balcony bra. I unhook her bra and kiss her nipples, and she gets to work unbuttoning my fly.

'So what are we going to do?' I ask, a little nervously.

'I want my boy to fuck me,' she says.

I wriggle out of my jeans and my darling unbuttons my shirt, trailing her hand down my stomach and over the tops of my arms, ignoring my bound breasts entirely, though my nipples long for attention. She draws a pattern of kisses over my thighs, and begins to masturbate the dildo, which then vibrates against my clitoris. It's an odd feeling, but it feels almost like it is a part of me, the way

217

she treats it – but then, my darling has some acting training as well, so it's not surprising. Somehow the whole mime stops just short of feeling absurd, and I think it's mostly that I'm so turned on it almost hurts, with my darling half on top of me and kissing me and pleasuring me in a way that's altogether new. Add to that the start I get every time I see the reflection of my face.

She half-unhooks the strap-on so she can replace the dildo with a firmer one, which it turns out she'd already got ready on the bedside table. This one doesn't vibrate but now she's slipping two fingers into my cunt, between the straps, filling the aching need that's there. She climbs back on top of me, pushes the dildo inside herself and begins to ride on it; slow, sensual, bucking motions that make her moan, while all the time her fingers work inside me to make me come. I start to move faster against her, and though my cock is made of plastic it's almost like I can feel it inside her, when every movement makes the straps press against me in different ways, and she angles her fingers inside me to be in line with the rhythm of my fucking her.

She leans forward and lets me press my face into her breasts, lets me flick my tongue across her nipples. I kiss up to her neck and nip at the skin with my teeth, so she moans and thrusts a little harder against the dildo, the slightly rough back of the strap-on pressing against my clitoris as she does so. She grabs the back of my neck and, pulling me close into her shoulder, rolls us both over on the bed so now I'm on top, pushing my cock into her, harder and harder.

Also on the bedside table is a washcloth, and a small basin of water – my darling dabs the washcloth in the basin and then begins to wipe the make-up off my face. It's erotic in itself, her fingers tracing over my lips,

218

skimming the curve of my cheek. I slow down, but she murmurs, 'No – go harder,' so I do, I go harder still, our bodies bucking together as I shove my cock into her wet, willing cunt, feeling the wetness of my own cunt on my thighs, chafed by the straps that cup my arse.

My darling is gentle with my face, running the washcloth over it, then leaning in to kiss my lips. 'Close enough,' she says – I glance in the mirror to find I'm not exactly make-up free, but nor do I look like a boy any more. I fuck her harder. I feel sexy, this odd, in-between version of myself, breasts bound flat, plunging my hard cock into my darling. Her moans are interspersed with little cries as I change the angle I'm fucking her at, and her movements become still more hungry, more urgent, and I can feel that she's close to coming, those explosive orgasms of hers that always leave her spent and smiling.

Still, as we fuck she reaches to unpin the bandage around my chest, and slowly unwinds it from me. I don't make it easy; I run my thumb over her nipple, flicking it lightly with the nail, so she gasps and loses concentration for a moment. But she soon has the bandage loose, and flings it away into the bedroom. She cups my breasts almost reverently, running the tips of her fingers around the areolas, and placing a kiss in the middle of my cleavage.

'Don't slow down,' she gasps again.

'Don't be so distracting,' I mutter.

Her next few words are lost in breathy moans of pleasure. She grabs me and presses me against her while I fuck her, burying her face in my neck. She pulls the tie out of my hair, and it spills out in flowing curls over both of us as she comes, screaming her orgasm in my name against my neck, and holding me as tight as she can.

We look normal again, but my darling isn't done. She

loosens the straps and makes me clamber out of the strap-on, so she can move down the bed, between my legs, and begin to kiss and lick my clitoris. With all the pressure from the vibration and the strap-on, I respond to her touch almost instantly. She looks beautiful, still flushed from her own orgasm, burying her face in my cunt with enthusiasm. I moan, and she nips at my teeth, her hands cupping my arse, squeezing its curves. When I start to come I buck, and she holds my thighs firm, her tongue moving deliciously over me until all my need is satisfied, and she crawls up the bed again to hold me in her arms.

'My lady,' she says softly as she kisses me, 'my lady.'

Open House
by Elizabeth Coldwell

'So why don't you come over on Saturday, Lisa?' Karin asked, taking the last of her shopping from her car. 'It's open house.'

'Well, thanks, Karin. If you're sure.' In the three months since I'd been living at the side of her, I'd never so much as popped my head round her front door. In truth, I was surprised she'd even noticed I existed.

Karin Lindegard and I moved in very different circles, as the sleek silver Lexus parked on her drive and the shopping bags that stood by it, each bearing the name of an upmarket Knightsbridge department store, proved. Her cool Scandinavian looks, all ash-blonde hair and pointed cheekbones, had once bagged her a fabulously wealthy investment banker husband. When that marriage had ended, her husband conforming to every midlife crisis cliché by leaving her for a girl 20 years her junior, she'd screwed him for as much as she could in the divorce settlement. She'd been awarded the beautiful Fulham townhouse outside which we now stood, and enough money to keep her in designer outfits for the rest of her life. It was a lifestyle that couldn't have been more different than my own rather hand-to-mouth existence as a freelance illustrator. Currently, I was housesitting for my sister, Jo, and her husband, while he fulfilled an 18-

month work contract in Dubai. I'd watched Karin coming and going as I sat at my drawing board, but this was the first time we'd had any kind of conversation. Most of what I knew about her I'd learnt from her cleaner, Agneska, who I'd often bumped into while she was taking a sneaky cigarette break in the garden. Agneska loved to gossip, and thanks to her I knew all the comings and goings on Queensholme Road – who might be about to lose their job in the City, who was getting their kitchen remodelled, and who was fucking who behind whose back. All of it so much more interesting than my own life.

I thought about turning her down; Karin and I moved in such different circles, I couldn't see myself having anything in common with her, or any of her guests. But a night out would do me good; I'd been immersed in my latest commission for weeks – 50 illustrations of couples twined in impossibly athletic sex positions for a new guide to sensual lovemaking – and I needed to spend time around real people for once, rather than the erotic sketches and their photographic inspiration pinned to my drawing board. Proud as I was of those drawings, they couldn't fail to remind me how long it had been since I'd last been wrapped in the arms of a lover of my own.

'What time should I come round?' I asked.

'Oh, any time after eight will be fine.' Karen gathered up her bags and pushed open her wrought iron front gate.

'Do you need me to bring anything?'

She shook her head. 'Just yourself. That'll be all I need.'

Even so, when I rang her doorbell on Saturday evening I clutched a bottle of fizz, not wanting to turn up empty-handed. A shiny black SUV I'd never seen before was parked outside the house, and as I waited on the doorstep, the faint sound of music came from within. After a couple of moments, Karin answered the door, as stunning as I'd ever seen her. She was one of those women who could manage to look flawlessly groomed even when dressed in her jogging gear of baggy T-shirt and cycling shorts, but tonight, she wore a black sheath dress that emphasised the curves of her breasts and hips. The colour should have washed her out, given her fair hair and pale complexion, but somehow she looked radiant. If her husband thought he'd traded up when he'd left her, he must be a fool, I found myself thinking as she ushered me inside.

'Champagne, how nice,' Karin said, taking the bottle from me. 'And a very good year too. But you really shouldn't have, darling.'

'Oh, it's no trouble.' I shrugged, not wanting to confess that I'd taken it from Jo's wine cellar, in the hope she wouldn't notice it missing on her return. I didn't know exactly what impression Karin had gained of me during our brief conversation, but I suspected she'd have a hard time believing someone who lived on this street couldn't afford vintage champagne on a regular basis.

'Come through and I'll get you a drink, then introduce you to a few people.'

I followed her into the kitchen, admiring the room as Karin poured me a glass from a champagne bottle that already stood open on the counter. Like Jo, she appeared to have every top of the range appliance going, from the huge, American-style walk-in refrigerator to the gleaming cappuccino machine. I could only guess at how many of those appliances she ever used.

Once Karin had passed me my champagne, she led me through to the living room. My eyes were drawn to her bottom, outlined by the tight black dress. No sign of a panty line was visible I didn't usually have fantasies about other women, especially not ones in their 40s, but I'd had nothing but fit, gorgeous bodies on my mind ever since I'd started work on the illustrations for the sex manual. Karin would have been a perfect life model for my drawings, and I found myself wondering whether she had on a thong beneath that dress, and what she might look like with her bare moons divided by a thin strip of lace. I shook my head to clear it of the image as she began to introduce me to her guests.

When she'd called the event an "open house", I'd had flashbacks to parties in my student days, where no one was ever sure who'd formally been invited, who'd tagged along with friends, and who'd just heard music thumping out into the street and wandered inside to see what all the excitement was about. This couldn't have been more of a contrast to those crowded, raucous events that more often than not ended with couples occupying every bedroom for sex, some girl locked in the bathroom, crying, and the neighbours threatening to call the police if something wasn't done about the noise.

Less than a dozen people occupied Karin's living room, talking in murmurs and nibbling canapés. From hidden speakers, the *Summer* movement of Vivaldi's *Four Seasons* played at a low volume. I looked round, recognising a couple of the guests as living somewhere on this street; I regularly saw the middle-aged redhead who now perched on the sofa walking her Bichon Frisé past my window as I sat at my drawing board. I'd half hoped Agneska would be here, so I'd have at least one friendly face to chat to, but I supposed it wasn't the done thing to socialise with one's help. Civilised as all this might have been, if this was an open house, I'd thought I'd hate to see a closed one.

Wandering over to the table, I helped myself to a blini topped with sour cream and caviar. My usual Saturday night involved slumping on the sofa in front of the latest TV talent show with a takeaway pizza and a glass of wine. One bite of my blini told me Karin's catering was a definite step or six above that culinary level.

As I reached for a small square of Welsh Rarebit on rye, I heard a deep, masculine voice behind me. 'I don't think I've seen you at one of Karin's soireés before.'

Turning, I found myself looking into a pair of brown eyes. Their owner was somewhere around 40, his dark hair styled with gel and the neat cut of his suit offset by having his top shirt button left open. His gaze raked up and down my body in a slow, assessing motion.

'I'm Lisa,' I told him. 'I live next door.'

'Oh, you're Jo's sister. Well, I'm Alec. Lovely to meet you.' He took a pace closer. I smelled citrus aftershave and well-groomed male. 'So how is she, and William?'

'They're both fine. I think they're finding the ex-pat life a little boring, but –' I shrugged, less concerned with making small talk about my sister than working out whether this suave, handsome man was coming on to me.

His next words wiped away any doubts I might have had about that. 'That's a charming dress you have on, Lisa. But it would look even nicer off.' As he spoke, his eyes hovered somewhere around my cleavage; I felt like the layers of cotton and lace I wore were being stripped from me, so he could feast on my naked breasts. 'Why don't we go somewhere a little more private, get to know each other better?'

Unseen by any of the other guests, Alec placed a caressing hand on my bottom. He might have been a fast worker but his touch felt good, and I would have responded to his illicit invitation in a heartbeat, if Karin hadn't joined us at that moment.

'Ah, Alec. There you are. Grace was looking for you; I think she's out in the garden if you'd like to join her.'

A dark, glowering expression crossed Alec's face. 'Maybe later, Lisa?' he said, before he strode off in the direction of the half-open French windows that let out on to Karin's garden.

'Who's Grace?' I asked, not recalling having met anyone of that name.

'Alec's wife,' Karin said grimly. 'I'm sorry, Lisa, but the man's the biggest lech on the street, and he has a nose for fresh meat.'

'Thanks for warning me.' I took a sip of my drink, realising to my surprise that the glass was already empty.

'Let me top that up for you,' Karin suggested.

'Actually, I think I'd like to use the bathroom first.' My cheeks were burning hot with embarrassment at how easily I'd been sucked in by Alec's charm, and I wanted to take a moment to splash cold water on my face and compose myself.

'OK, I'll show you where it is.'

Karin led me out into the hall and up the stairs. As I followed her, my gaze was again drawn to the hypnotic sway of her buttocks. What was happening to me? I'd just had a narrow escape from the clutches of an apparent serial philanderer, and now I was having lustful thoughts about my next-door neighbour. Maybe my body was just reacting to being let off the leash of a tight work deadline, but I couldn't imagine Karin would be too thrilled to know I was dreaming of peeling the dress from her and burying my face between the cheeks of her arse.

She pushed open the bathroom door and flipped the light switch. A fan began to whirr softly as the light came on. I expected her to withdraw and leave me to my ablutions, but she didn't. Instead, she stepped into the bathroom with me.

'It's OK, Karin, I should be fine now,' I told her.

'I'm sure you will,' she said, pushing the door softly shut. 'I just needed you to know what kind of man Alec was before you did anything you might regret.'

'Thanks,' I told her sincerely. 'I really appreciate it. I've always had a rule that I don't get involved with married men.'

'Anyone else you don't get involved with?' Suddenly, she seemed to be much nearer to me than before, close enough that I was all too aware of the heat of her skin and the subtle, earthy scent of her. For all that she was exquisitely groomed, she hadn't bothered with perfume, and everything I could smell was pure woman.

'I – I …' My words died in my throat as Karin ran a manicured fingernail along my arm.

'You've never been with a woman, have you?' Her voice was a sensual purr. 'But I can tell you're not averse to the idea. You're … curious.'

From nowhere, the word "cougar" popped into my head. The older, experienced woman seducing her prey. How many times had she done this before? If I said yes, would I be just another notch on her bedpost?

'Don't worry,' she said, as if sensing my anxiety. 'I'm not like Alec. Chasing women is force of habit with him; I don't know how Grace puts up with it. I like girls, Lisa, but I only make a move on the ones I really like. The special ones …'

I'd never imagined the evening would take this kind of turn; if I'd entertained any fantasies at all about hooking up with someone, they certainly hadn't involved my hostess, or a seduction in a bathroom that wouldn't have looked out of place in an exclusive spa. But now, as Lisa pulled me into an embrace, I didn't resist. She was right; I was curious. Part of me ached to know how it would feel to have her lips on mine, or for that cool, pink-painted mouth to latch onto my nipple and suck …

'Just relax,' she murmured. 'Let me take care of everything.'

Her mouth came down on mine; I tasted lipstick and champagne, felt the softness of her lips pressing against my own. Karin's kiss overwhelmed me. On some level I'd known it would be different to kissing a man – no prick of stubble, no male scent in my nostrils – but the reality was better than I could ever have imagined. I closed my eyes and surrendered to her gentle caresses.

By the time we pulled apart, my lips tingled and my breathing was shallow, excited. I'd almost forgotten there was a cocktail party happening downstairs – a party that was missing its hostess. Karin didn't seem to care about leaving her guests unattended, too busy reaching for the zip of my dress and pulling it down. Between us, we pushed the sleeves off my shoulders, and I let the dress fall to the floor.

Karin smiled in approval, and I thanked my foresight in choosing to wear one of my prettiest sets of underwear tonight, a pale blue bra and matching boy shorts.

'Very cute,' she said, as she removed her own dress. I couldn't believe my naughty imaginings had been correct; she was indeed wearing a skimpy thong – and nothing else. Her tits were surprisingly firm, given their size. She caught me staring. 'Nice, aren't they? Michael certainly thought so, though he paid enough to get them looking this way.'

With that, she guided me down to the bathroom floor. The tiles felt warmer against my back than I'd expected.

Karin chuckled at my reaction. 'Michael paid for the underfloor heating too. When we have more time, I'll give you a guided tour of the whole house, but for now there are more important things.'

She straddled me with her toned thighs, facing away so we were top to tail. I had a delicious view of her bum, the thin crotch of her thong moulded to her pussy lips, as she worked to remove my panties. I let my thighs loll open, knowing instinctively what her next move would be. After all, I was dying to lick her, and I knew she'd want to do the same, given her view of my cunt was so much ruder. I was wet, shamefully so, and she bent her head so she could swipe her tongue along my juicy split. Just that touch had me shuddering beneath her, and I realised how much I needed this. All work and no play had left me hungering for a skilled lover – and Karin had skill to burn.

She tasted me like I was a fine wine, lapping up my nectar as it flooded out of me. The tip of her tongue traced the seam of my sex lips, pushing between them so she could lick my clit. My fevered response was to hook the thin strip of fabric covering her pussy to one side, so I could lick her in return. The fan still thrummed in the background, white noise that didn't mask the sounds of our moans.

My hips humped against the floor as I sought to push my pussy harder against Karin's mouth. As beautiful as her soft oral caresses felt, I missed the sensation of being filled.

'Need – need your fingers inside me,' I managed to tell her, breaking off from eating her cunt just long enough to phrase my request.

'For you, honey, anything.' With that, two slender fingers pushed past the soaking rim of my pussy. When Karen curved those digits upwards, striking the sweet, hidden spot high up on my pussy wall, I lost it, thrashing beneath her as she stroked me towards ecstasy.

The door handle rattled. I froze in mid-lick. Had Karin locked the bathroom door? If someone burst in on us now, I didn't know how I'd react. I could only imagine the view they'd have, with Karin's head buried between my wide-spread legs, busily lapping away.

'It's occupied.' Karin sounded remarkably composed for a woman about to be caught in the act of lesbian love. 'You can use the en suite in my bedroom if you need to.'

Holding my breath, I prayed whoever was seeking to gain entry would do as Karin suggested. To the relief, I was sure, of both of us, there was no further attempt to get inside.

'We don't have much time,' Karin muttered, as she began thrusting her fingers deep in my hole once more.

'That's OK, we don't need it,' I replied between gasping breaths. She was touching me in all the places that counted, and I knew I was close. The way she wriggled, forcing her bottom down hard onto my mouth, made me think her orgasm couldn't be far off either.

I didn't care which of us came first, only that my satisfaction – and Karin's – was swift and sweet. Rolling, tumbling, touching, tasting, we fell headlong into orgasm almost as one. My cunt convulsed around her probing fingers, and her pussy gushed its juice into my eagerly sucking mouth. The heady scent of her enveloped me, and I clung tight to her as our pleasure crested before slowly subsiding.

At last, we came back to some realisation of where we were, and of where we should be. Karin grabbed her dress. As she zipped herself back into it, I had to admire the fact that a slight smudging of her lipstick was the only outward indication of the hot, passionate encounter we'd just shared. I would need a little longer to put myself back into a respectable state, and I told her so.

'That's fine, Lisa. After all, it might look a little suspicious if we came back to the party together.' She smiled at me. 'When you get back downstairs, there'll be fresh champagne waiting for you. I'd better go and check on the guests, make sure they haven't been bitching about me in my absence.'

Once more she was my cool, controlled, sophisticated neighbour, almost as if what we'd just done had been a mere distraction from the real events of the evening. I bit back the disappointment I couldn't help but feel at her eagerness to be out of the room.

Then she paused with her hand on the door handle. 'And don't forget I have a tour of the house planned for you. You'll like my bedroom, Lisa. My bed is … very comfortable.'

And that's when I realised her open house event was by no means over. Indeed, for me, it was only just beginning.

Also from Xcite Books

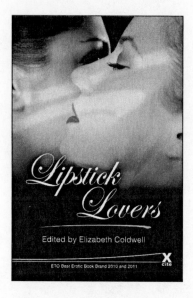

Lipstick Lovers

In this sizzling selection of twenty erotic lesbian stories, find out what happens when women act on their overwhelming lust for each other. Dominant mistresses and willing slaves, bi-curious best friends, strangers swept away by the thrill of passion, and long-time lovers spicing up their sex lives, share the pages of *Lipstick Lovers*.

Explicit fantasy and naughty adventures make this the hottest lesbian collection from the best writers in the genre.

Everyone has fun when girls come together.

ISBN 9781908086686

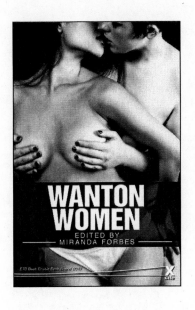

Wanton Women

Twenty hot tales about ladies who lust... after each other.
From vulnerable virgins to femme fatales to misbehaving
minxes, these wanton women all have one thing in
common. They don't need a man to satisfy them in bed –
or anywhere else for that matter! Wild women or just girls
getting it on, these stories are guaranteed to tease.

ISBN 9781907761683

Please review me – thank you!

**To join our mailing list
please scan the QR code**